BREAKING RULES

THE SCOTTISH BILLIONAIRE BOOK 2

M. S. PARKER

BELMONTE PUBLISHING, LLC

THE SCOTTISH BILLIONAIRE READING ORDER

Thank you for reading *Breaking Rules*, the second book in my new series, *The Scottish Billionaire*. I highly recommend reading the books in this order:

Prequel – The Scottish Billionaire
1. Off Limits
2. Breaking Rules (This book)
3. Mending Fate (Coming June 9th)

ONE

ALEC

THE DAY WAS RAINY AND OVERCAST, BARELY OVER fifty degrees, which made it a completely average Monday afternoon at the beginning of October. Well, in Seattle, Washington, anyway. For someone with my control issues and need for continuity, it was perfect. For someone from Scotland, it felt like home.

I'd come to the States as a child, but an old enough one to remember where I came from. I remembered becoming a US citizen, but I'd kept my Scottish citizenship too. I didn't know if any of my siblings had kept theirs. I'd been the only one who'd returned to Scotland for university, but since receiving my degree, I'd only gone back for work.

Maybe it was time to plan a trip I could take my daughter on, let her see where her grandparents – the

1

grand-da she knew, as well as the gran she didn't – had met and fallen in love, where I had been born and spent the first nine years of my life.

Evanne would love it. I'd never taken a vacation in all my years as CEO of my family's company, MIRI. A month over the next summer might be just the thing. And if it was summer, perhaps Evanne's teacher could join us.

My dick pulsed at that thought.

"Mr. McCrae!" My assistant, Tuesday Boswell, burst into my office just as I was shifting in my chair. "Turn on the TV!"

I stared at her in complete surprise, my hard-on fading as quickly as it had come. Tuesday was the most level-headed, professional woman I'd ever met. Da himself had picked her out to be my assistant when I'd started at MIRI. She'd never come in without knocking or buzzing the intercom.

"I'm sorry, Mr. McCrae," she said as she hurried over to the television I kept in the corner for emergencies, "but this is important."

Only the fact that I knew she wasn't one given to dramatics kept me from reprimanding her. She grabbed the remote and turned from the business report being presented to a local channel.

The moment I saw what was on the screen, I forgot that Tuesday had interrupted my lunch.

"...a series of gunshots at Kurt Wright School. Police are on the scene..."

I didn't wait to hear anything else or to see anything more than a helicopter shot of the school. My daughter and the woman I...Lumen...I had to go.

Immediately.

I grabbed my car keys and phone, shoving the latter into my pocket as I practically ran to the elevator. My heart thudded against my ribcage, and the thoughts that raced through my mind piled up on each other, each one worse than the last, something I wouldn't have thought possible. If I'd been thinking at all.

It took every ounce of self-control I possessed to keep from speeding through the streets. I had always prided myself on my ability to adhere to a strict schedule without needing to break speed limits and the like. This, however, was no simple meeting to which I was running late.

There had been gunshots at my daughter's school.

The tragedy and horror that had plagued this nation for too long had finally struck my home. If an elite private school, funded by Seattle's wealthiest and most influential inhabitants, couldn't keep our children safe, could anywhere? How could we keep letting this happen?

The street was already closed off, Seattle PD's finest lining up behind barriers and police tape. Cars were jam-packed and double-parked, more than half with drivers who looked right pissed at how impossible it was going to be to get out of here.

As much as panic tried to take over, I managed to keep my head long enough to find a parking spot another street over. I'd probably get a ticket, but that wasn't important. I ran back to the line, ears straining to hear another shot. All I heard, however, were the shouts of the people who wanted to know where their kids were and if anyone had been hurt.

Excellent questions.

When I was in sight of the barricade, I slowed to a walk, not because I was any less anxious, but because if there was one thing I knew, it was how important appearance was. If I looked like I was in control, they'd be more likely to listen to me than if I looked to be a panicked parent.

The chaos inside had to stay hidden.

"Excuse me!" I shouted at one of the cops, pushing my way through the crowd. I'd never been so glad to be six-and-a-half feet tall as I was now. I doubted people would have moved out of my way as fast if I'd been a smaller man.

"I can't let you through, sir." The cop's eyes widened as I reached the police tape. "Everything is under control, and statements will be made when the authorities deem it appropriate."

"Don't you be givin' me the party line." The one thing I couldn't control as well as I could my expression was my accent. The more keyed up I was, the thicker it became. "I have a daughter in there."

And a...lover? I didn't know what Lumen was, exactly, but only Evanne was more important right now.

"I understand, but I have my orders." The kid's voice shook, and I almost felt sorry for him.

Almost.

I narrowed my eyes, leaning closer to him. "What. Happened."

"Someone said it was firecrackers." A woman next to me spoke up. "But those weren't firecrackers."

"Are you a parent?" I asked the question even though I doubted this woman had the means to send a child to this particular institution.

"I'm a janitor," she said, lifting her chin. "Afternoon shift. I was one of the people who called 911. I know gunshots when I hear them. I grew up in Youngstown."

I squeezed her arm, thankful for the information and her quick thinking. "How many gunshots did you hear?"

"Six."

"There were three." An older man with an ascot stood off to the side, a sour expression on his face. "And I've been informed that the suspect is in custody."

It took me a moment to place who he was. "Mr. Arkham, right?"

"You're the McCrae boy."

I was in my early thirties, which meant I couldn't really be a boy, but I wasn't about to argue that when I wanted answers. "Alec McCrae, aye. You have answers about what happened?"

"No one knows anything," the cop interrupted. "You have to wait until an announcement is made."

"I am not waitin' to see my daughter," I said firmly, working to keep my voice even. "Or to find out if she's hurt."

"I heard two people were taken to the hospital." A well-dressed woman was wringing her hands as she paced. "At least tell us if they were kids or adults. My Spencer is in there. Please. Tell us something."

"I have a friend on the force," Mr. Arkham said. "The ambulance was for a teacher who fainted and hit their head."

For a moment, Lumen's face popped into my mind,

but I pushed it away. If she was hurt, it wouldn't have been from passing out. The lass was one of the strongest people I'd ever met.

When the cop still refused to speak, the people behind me started shouting.

"We need to get in there!"

"Stop stalling!"

"What the hell's going on in there?!"

"Those are our kids!"

"Do you know who I am?!"

"I'll have your badge!"

The cop shifted, glancing around him as if looking for assistance, but all the way around the perimeter, cops were dealing with the same thing.

I wasn't getting through here, but I wasn't giving up either. I hadn't gotten to where I was today by dropping things that were too hard. I started down the line, keeping close enough to the police tape that it moved as I walked. More than one person shouted at me for cutting in front of them, and the cops kept warning me back, but I ignored all of them. I ignored the stories flying around me too, not really caring what were rumors and what were facts. I'd learn what happened when I found Evanne and Lumen.

I finally spotted where the elementary students had been gathered and quickened my step. All my attention focused on the little figures, scanning for long, dark brown curls and the blue bow I'd put in her hair this morning. She was tall for her age, but still only eight, so I worried that I wouldn't be able to see her over the older kids and adults.

Then I saw a familiar slender body and thick, honey-blonde waves pulled back from a face I'd had in my mind for nearly two full months. As she turned, I spotted a figure clinging to her, and everything else disappeared.

"Evanne!"

TWO
LUMEN

I JOTTED MYSELF A NOTE TO PUT GREEN PEPPERS ON the grocery list that Mai and I had hanging on our fridge and then added to the note that we needed to decide who was going grocery shopping this week. I supposed it'd come down to whether I'd spend more time with Alec and Evanne, or if Mai would spend more with Hob. Then again, the less time I was at the apartment, the more time my roommate could have with her boyfriend in the privacy of our home.

I just hoped that wouldn't turn into another instance of me walking in on the two of them having sex on our couch. I was still trying to get over the last time I'd found the two of them naked. It wasn't something I wanted to see again.

I picked up the last crisp pepper slice from the

vegetable portion of my lunch and bit it in half. In the silence of my classroom, the crunching sound I made while chewing was louder than I'd realized it would be. Or maybe the kids had just been noisier than usual today. I loved my students, but I also loved having this small bit of time to myself in the middle of the–

My phone buzzed from inside my purse, but by the time I dug it out, it was too late. I frowned as I saw Soleil's name pop up on my screen. It wasn't that I minded her calling me. Hell, I'd given her my number in the hopes that she would *call. But it was the middle of the day, and she should have been in school. Why would she have called when she should be in class?*

I still had a few minutes before I had to go get my class, so I tapped Soleil's name to call her back. The phone rang once. Twice–

A loud bang startled me into nearly dropping my phone.

That couldn't have been what–

A second bang left no doubt in my mind what I was hearing.

Gunshots.

"Evanne!"

The shout pulled me out of the memory. My heart was racing, but it'd started racing after the first gunshot and hadn't stopped since. We'd had a whole section of our pre-beginning-of-the-year meeting dedicated to active shooter drills, but we hadn't run one yet.

Since my kids had been in the lunchroom at the time, I'd known where they'd be taken for the meeting point and had made my way there once I'd confirmed that my hallway was empty. The kids were confused and a little upset, but none of them were freaking out, which made me wonder how much they actually knew about what'd happened.

Hell, *I* didn't know what had happened.

"Evanne!"

I turned, taking Evanne with me. I knew that voice, and my eyes immediately sought out the person who went with it. Alec's golden blond hair was easy to spot, and the moment my eyes met his, the panic I'd been feeling faded. I could still see his in those bright blue eyes, though, and I knew he wouldn't relax until he had his arms around his daughter.

I turned slightly, motioning to the lunch monitor who'd brought the kids out. "That's Evanne's dad." I pointed. "Alec McCrae."

Her eyes widened, letting me know that she knew the name. Good. He wasn't one to use his name to get special privileges, but I had a scared little girl hugging me, and a dad who was probably even more frightened than she was.

"I'm going to take Evanne to her father," I said.

"We're supposed to keep the kids until Principal McKenna dismisses us."

My laugh was more snort than anything. "Trust me, Principal McKenna cares more about making Mr. McCrae happy than he does about following the rules. She's already been marked as accounted for, and if anyone has any issues, I'll take responsibility for it."

The look on the lunch monitor's face assured me that if there was trouble, I would indeed be the one taking responsibility for any complaints. I gave her a small smile before putting my head closer to Evanne's.

"Hey, sweetie, your dad's here."

Her head came up, pretty blue eyes wide. "He is?"

"I'm going to take you over to him, okay?"

She nodded, and the two of us made our way over to where Alec was impatiently waiting on the other side of the police tape. I almost felt sorry for the cop standing nearby, knowing Alec had probably been giving him a hard time about not being allowed to come get Evanne. The guy was just doing his job, but if I'd learned anything at all about Alec in the short time I'd known him, it was that he didn't let anything get in the way of what he wanted...and his daughter was at the top of that list.

"Daddy!" Evanne ducked under the tape before the cop could even turn completely toward us.

"Miss..."

I held up a hand. "I'm her teacher, Ms. Browne, and I'm releasing her to her father's custody."

"*Mo chride*," Alec murmured as he hugged Evanne. The rest of what he said either wasn't in English or was said with an accent too thick for me to understand.

"If these parents start demanding their kids back too, can I send them to you?" the cop asked, clearly annoyed.

"Vargas!" Another cop gestured to the one getting ready to argue with me. "We got orders!"

"Thank you, lass," Alec said, drawing my attention back to him as the cop walked away. "I was going mad. What happened?"

Before I could answer, someone called my name. A few feet away, Soleil Artz ducked around an angry woman who seemed to be threatening a cop if he didn't let her cut through the school parking lot to get to where her car was parked rather than having to walk around the block. I suddenly remembered that Soleil had called me right before I'd heard the gunshots.

"I need to go," I said to Alec.

He didn't answer, but I understood. Evanne was foremost on his mind at the moment, and I wouldn't have cared so much about him if his daughter hadn't been his priority. He'd reach out once Evanne was settled, and we knew more about what had happened.

I stayed on my side of the police tape but moved down the line until Soleil was directly across from me. "What are you doing here?"

"I heard someone had a gun." Soleil shuffled her feet, her hazel eyes refusing to meet mine. "I was curious."

"'Curious?'" I raised an eyebrow. "It's okay to say you were worried. If I heard there'd been a shooting at your school, I'd be worried for you."

She shrugged, not giving an inch.

"You called me but didn't leave a message."

"You didn't answer."

Was that what had prompted Soleil coming here, wanting to know why I hadn't picked up? "I couldn't get to my phone in time, but I was getting ready to call you back when the shooting started. Are you okay?"

Her mouth quirked up at the corners, but only for a moment. "I'm fine."

I reached across the police tape and lightly touched Soleil's arm. She looked at me. "You called me on a school day, and now you're here instead of in school. What's going on?"

"It's nothing."

The stubborn set of her jaw told me I wouldn't get

much of anything else from her. Still, I wasn't about to just let her walk off because the conversation was finished. Something was on her mind, and despite what had just happened at my place of work, whatever was going on with her was important enough to take precedence. My students were all safe. There was nothing more I could do here.

"Wait right here," I instructed. "I'm going to check with the principal about what we're supposed to do next. If I have to stay, you can stay with me, and either way, we'll take a Lyft back to the house before I go home."

Soleil opened her mouth to protest, but I held up a finger and shook my head. I waited until she grumbled an unhappy *okay* before leaving her there. The anxiety and fear that had been coursing through me from the moment I'd recognized the gunshots for what they were receded. I had a purpose, and that would help me keep my emotions under control until I was alone.

It was easy to find Principal McKenna. Half a dozen other teachers and aides were already crowded around him. Vice Principal Cornelius Harvey, fortunately, was nowhere to be seen. The last thing I needed right now was to have to deal with his lechery. As I stepped in between the kindergarten aide and the art teacher, I found that at least a couple of the questions I had were being answered.

"...so, no, we're not sure what happened. We do know that no one was hurt, other than a few bumps and bruises. Until a full investigation is completed, the school will be closed. Once you've confirmed attendance, please send an aide to me with your attendance sheet, and then we can begin releasing students. Once your class is released, please find an officer and give them your statement. They've been instructed that all student statements are to be taken at the discretion of that student's guardian."

I waited until the others moved off to do their necessary tasks before speaking up. "Principal McKenna, I have a young woman who I'm sort of a big sister to. She's only fourteen. May I bring her inside the police tape to wait until I'm able to take her home?"

For a moment, I thought he'd refuse, but then he nodded. "Just make sure the police know and don't let her wander."

"Yes, sir. Thank you." I headed back toward where Soleil was waiting. I supposed I could have just gotten her a ride alone, but if I made her wait until we could both go, it'd give me more time to figure out what was going on with her.

HAVING extra time with Soleil only helped when she actually talked, which meant by the time the car pulled up in front of the group home where I'd once lived, I'd spent an additional hour with her and still hadn't learned anything about what had caused her to call me in the middle of the day, or why she'd been out of school. In fact, she'd barely said a word at all, though she had asked if I was okay after I'd given my statement to one of the harried-looking cops standing inside the marked off area.

"Do you need me to come talk to Brie?" I asked as the driver put the car into park. "Let her know where you've been?"

Soleil shook her head. "She's not home. Kim had some sort of all-day thing. Brie had to go with her."

"Is it something serious?"

"I don't think so." She opened the door. "Thanks."

The door was closed before I could say anything else. I asked the driver to wait until she went inside, though, before I had him go. The ride back to my place was quiet, but at least I wasn't alone. I hadn't been alone since it'd happened, and for the first time, I was glad my budget hadn't yet allowed for a car. I wasn't sure I would've been safe to drive myself after what'd happened. As it was, I struggled to keep my thoughts from straying back to those horrible moments.

"I didn't want to ask you when that girl was in the car, but were you guys at the school when that shooting happened?" The driver glanced in the rearview mirror, his eyes meeting mine for a second before going back to the road. "I heard something about it on the news."

"I'm a teacher at Kurt Wright," I admitted, "but we don't know yet what happened. There's an investigation."

"Well, I hope they catch whoever did it. One of these days, a politician is going to lose one of their kids or grandkids, and that's when things will finally change." Apparently, this was a topic he felt strongly about because he continued to talk the entire rest of the way.

At least he wasn't some conspiracy theorist or someone coming up with some crazy solution that couldn't possibly work. If it'd happened somewhere else, I might've even joined in the discussion, but I couldn't even really let myself hear it, not without losing control over what I was feeling.

Then, finally, I was home. I handed him a couple folded bills, told him to keep the change, and then hurried into the building. The sound of my feet on the stairs sent my heart racing, sending my mind back to how I'd imagined hearing someone coming after me as I'd made my way down the hall toward the nearest exit.

I'd wanted to go to the cafeteria. Get to my kids and

protect them. But I'd remembered how we'd been told what we were to do if we were alone in this type of situation. We weren't supposed to deviate from the plan in place. No heroics. Over and over, it'd been emphasized how we could put people in danger if we didn't do what we were supposed to do.

I'd hated every second, but the anger at my helplessness had managed to drive away the majority of my fear. I'd at least found my class quickly, because if I hadn't, I wasn't sure I would've been able to stop myself from going back inside.

The second I opened my door, I realized there was someone I should have called as soon as I had a chance.

"Lumen!" Mai threw her arms around me, nearly knocking me off my feet.

I grabbed at the door, managing to shut it behind us because it didn't seem like she was going to let go anytime soon.

"I was so worried! Hob heard about it at work because they let all the hospitals know, and he called me." Her arms tightened around me. "Are you okay?"

"I'm fine." I put my hands on her shoulders and pulled her back a bit. "I wasn't hurt. I didn't even see anything."

Mei's eyes narrowed as she stepped back. "If you weren't hurt, then where have you been?"

"I had to give my statement to the police and make sure my students got to their parents." I set my bag down and toed off my shoes, sighing in relief. "Plus, Soleil showed up, and I had to take her back to the home."

"And you couldn't be bothered to take the time to send a text to let me know you weren't dead or dying?"

The hurt in Mai's voice cut me and the tears I'd managed to keep back welled up instantly. "I'm so sorry. I didn't think...I mean, it was crazy, and I just kept thinking about the next thing I had to do. I'm not used to having someone care that much–"

"Of course I care! I didn't mean to make you feel bad," Mai said, hugging me again. "I was just terrified that something had happened to you."

"I'll do better," I promised. "The next time I'm in a life-threatening situation, I'll reach out."

I made the comment light, but the sentiment was genuine. Emotion nearly choked me, and I knew I needed to get out of there as quickly as possible.

"I don't mean to be rude, but I really need to get a shower," I said as I forced a small smile. "It's been a long day."

"Take your time," Mai said, already reaching for her phone. "I'll order us some dinner."

I nodded, not trusting my voice. As soon as she let me go, I hurried to the bathroom. The moment I shut the door, the damn broke, and I slapped a hand over my mouth to stifle the sob that came out of me.

I turned on the shower and then let go. Tears streamed down my face as I undressed, but I no longer tried to stop them. If my childhood and adolescence had taught me anything, it was how to cry in a shower without letting anyone know that's what you were doing.

THREE
ALEC

THE TIGHT GRIP I ALWAYS HELD ON MY EMOTIONS was threatening to crack. I always had the answers, knew the right things to do or say. On the rare occasions I didn't know, I had the means and the drive to find someone who did.

Now though, I was at a loss.

I'd never imagined that this sort of thing could happen at my daughter's school. Then again, I'd never actually thought about it at all. School had been Keli's thing to handle. I'd just assumed that she'd made certain that Kurt Wright was safe.

Common sense said I should wait until I found out what really happened *before* I made any rash decisions. Like taking Evanne out of school entirely and hiring a tutor to homeschool her so she'd never have to leave the house.

Better idea.

If I hired Lumen as the tutor, I could keep them *both* safely locked away.

Somehow, I doubted either of them would appreciate it very much if I followed through.

Evanne, however, didn't have to like it. I'd do what was best for her, even if she was furious with me. Lumen...she was something else.

"Am I going to have school tomorrow?" she asked as we pulled into the driveway. "We were supposed to have a spelling test after lunch, and I studied for it."

"I don't know, sweetheart," I said, resisting the impulse to tell her that she wasn't going back to that school anytime soon. I needed to wait and see, make an informed decision that would be the best thing for my daughter.

I also needed to figure out when and what I was going to tell Keli. My gut said she would find a way to make this my fault somehow.

"Someone did something bad, didn't they?" Evanne asked as I unlocked the door and then reset the alarm code.

"What makes you say that?" I asked, heart squeezing painfully.

What had she seen? Heard?

Evanne shrugged. "I just thought that must've been what happened because all the teachers looked angry like they do when kids are bad."

I wasn't sure if I wanted to know the answer to the question I was about to ask, but I had to ask it. I had to know. "What happened today?"

"Well, we had a math quiz, and I did really good on it. Then we learned about—"

"I meant during lunch." I really hoped her automatic assumption that I wanted to hear about her whole day meant whatever had happened hadn't made a lasting impression.

"Oh, *that*." She headed for the kitchen, and I followed. "Well, I was eating mac 'n cheese and somebody dropped something two times. Or dropped two things. The teachers and lunch aides got real quiet, like they were mad, and then they told us all to line up. We weren't done eating, but they said we had to go outside right away."

Somebody had dropped something.

"I think there were spiders and snakes."

I blinked, confused by the apparent change of subject. "Where were there snakes and spiders, *mo chride*?"

"I think that's why we had to go outside," she said

matter-of-factly. "I think someone dropped some boxes with snakes and spiders in them, and that's why we had to leave."

My eyebrows shot up. She had quite the imagination, my daughter. "Spiders and snakes."

She nodded solemnly. "That's why I was scared in the parking lot. I didn't want them to get out and bite anyone."

"You're not scared now, then?"

She shook her head. "I knew we didn't have any in our car so we're safe now."

On occasion, a child's logic actually made a wee bit of sense. "Did you ask Ms. Browne about what happened?"

"No. She was busy when she found us."

"Found you? She wasn't with you already?" My temper flared.

"It wasn't her turn to be in the cafeteria with us." Evanne skipped to the kitchen. "Can I have a snack?"

Lumen had left my daughter alone. I frowned as I followed Evanne. Lumen hadn't simply left *my* child, though. She'd left all of them. Her job was to take care of the children under her charge, and she'd simply been somewhere else. How could she have done that?

"What do you want?" I asked, opening the refrigerator. "Do all of the teachers leave their classes when it's time to eat?"

"I didn't get my dessert at lunch," she informed me seriously. "I want a cookie."

"All right." I reached for the box of shortbread cookies Theresa had sent to us a few days ago. "But just two."

"Okay," she agreed. "And yes."

"Yes?"

"The other teachers, when it's not their turn to have lunch with us, they go somewhere else. I don't know where."

My annoyance at Lumen faded as quickly as it'd come. It'd been foolish of me to think she'd been neglecting her duties. This entire situation had sent my brain into a tailspin. I was doubting people who had done nothing to deserve that doubt.

The text tone for my phone broke me from my thoughts. The message on the screen answered one question, at least.

"It looks like school is canceled for the rest of the week." I didn't add the explanation that the text had contained, that the police were investigating what had happened, and that the school would be offering counseling at a place to be determined at a later date. There were no known injuries and no other details being released at this time.

"That sucks." Evanne stuck out her bottom lip.

"*Mo chride.*" I made my tone a warning one. "You know your mother doesn't like you saying that."

"Sorry," Evanne said, "but there's nothing else that describes how I feel."

The serious and overly dramatic statement was enough to make me crack a smile. There was a reason I used the endearment *mo chride* for my daughter. It meant *my heart,* and that was what she was. She was everything.

"What would you say about going to visit your grandparents for the next few days?"

"Yay!" Evanne threw her hands up in the air. "When?"

"I'll need to make a couple calls, but I believe we can leave tonight."

"I'll go pack."

With that, she ran off. I'd need to go through her bags before we left and make sure she wasn't taking only toys. She had plenty of those at her grandparents' house.

Before I called for a private plane, I had one other person I had to contact.

"Text Lumen." I waited a moment and then continued with my voice-to-text, "'Evanne and I are going to visit my parents for the week. I'll let you know when we're back.'"

Maybe it was a bit abrupt, but this wasn't exactly a normal situation. That was what I needed, what going home would provide. Normalcy. A solid place with solid people where Evanne and I could find our footing again.

FOUR
LUMEN

EVANNE AND I ARE GOING TO VISIT MY PARENTS FOR the week. I'll let you know when we're back.

I read it again, now half-convinced that I had some sort of masochistic tendencies since the only thing that re-reading accomplished was annoying me more. I tried not to be hurt.

It was nice of him to let me know what was going on, after all. I wasn't his girlfriend, not exactly, anyway. Sure, he'd given me a key to his place, and we hadn't discussed labels, and we weren't at a point where we had to let each other know what we were doing all the time.

Maybe the key was why he'd told me at all. If I hadn't known they were going away, I might've shown up at the house and found them gone. Alec texting me that they were going out of town for a little while was courtesy that he hadn't needed to extend.

All of that reasoning, however, didn't make me less hurt that he'd decided to take Evanne and go without even asking me how I was doing. I understood his initial concern being entirely focused on his daughter, but it would've been nice to have gotten a simple 'how are you?'

That thought was followed by a rush of guilt every single time. I hadn't been injured. Hell, I hadn't even seen what had happened. I'd heard some gunshots. That was it.

I'd been frightened, of course, but I was an adult, able to cope with the myriad emotions triggered by the event. Evanne was a child, and a child who'd recently been uprooted from her routine. That alone would've been enough to freak her out. For all I knew, Alec had spent the entire rest of the day comforting Evanne, and they were going to visit his parents so they could help him with the aftereffects of such a stressful day.

What sort of horrible person was upset with a man for taking care of his daughter?

Honestly, once I got my head out of my ass, I had to admit that if he hadn't put Evanne first, he would've lost some of my respect and admiration. A man whose daughter was his priority was actually, well, sexy. I knew all too well what it was like to *not* be the priority.

And I was going to be okay with it this time, I decided. I could handle this on my own. I'd handled everything else on my own. Evanne would never have to know what that felt like. She would grow up safe and become independent without the fear that came with never having a safety net. She might have to struggle with an overprotective father, but too much love must be better than too little.

I wouldn't know what one was like, but I knew the other well enough to know that it wasn't anything good.

Maybe what I needed to do was get my mind off things. Focus on something I could do. Someone I could help.

Soleil.

She hadn't said anything to me about why she'd called me in the first place, and she wasn't the sort of person I could push into revealing what was going on with her. She was wary, even more than I had been at her age. I'd gotten a shit hand in life, knocked around a time or two, went hungry more than I cared to remember, but my gut told me that this poor girl had been through more.

Evanne had Alec to support her, and while he was

doing that, I would offer my support to someone who needed it but didn't have anyone else. I wasn't Soleil's mother or sister or family in any way, but that didn't mean I couldn't be someone she could rely on and confide in. It would take time, but I was confident that I could eventually show her that she didn't have to go through life alone.

Maybe, one day, I'd accept the same about my own life.

FIVE

ALEC

Noise and voices woke me up, and for several seconds, I couldn't remember where I was.

Since Evanne had come to live with me, I'd come to give up my quiet life. I didn't miss it most of the time, even when privacy occasionally became...tricky. It hadn't taken long for me to recognize her sounds, though. What it was like when she got into the cabinets and refrigerator. The shows she watched. Her footsteps on the stairs.

These sounds didn't match.

They echoed strangely. Came through the floor in a way that didn't make sense. Only when I heard additional voices that I realized where I was and then remembered how I'd gotten here.

And why.

I rolled onto my back and stared up at the ceiling. My bedroom had become a guest room after I'd bought a place of my own. Actually, Theresa and Da had done that for each of us, giving us all a place to stay whenever we needed it, but without keeping our childhood bedrooms as unchanging shrines.

Evanne had a room of her own. As the only grand-child – a sore point for my very Catholic parents – she'd been spoiled from moment one. According to Da, Evanne would continue being spoiled until other grand-kids came along, but I had my doubts that the spoiling would ever stop. At least when the others finally started having kids, Da and Theresa would spoil mine less. I also planned to finally get revenge for the last eight years of loud presents and too much sugar.

By the time I made my way downstairs, breakfast was ready, and the kitchen table was crowded. When Da and Theresa had first bought this house, they'd knocked out a wall to expand the dining room and commissioned a massive table, adding chairs as we added new family members. Once we'd started moving out, they'd eventu-ally moved into the kitchen for 'small' gatherings. Considering there were sixteen of us, eighteen with Da and Theresa, 'small' was a relative term.

"Mornin'," I greeted the others.

"Bit of a late morning for you, isn't it?" Brody asked as I took the seat between him and Evanne. His blue-green eyes sparkled with good humor. A little under a year-and-a-half younger than me, we'd always been close. Some people thought it was in spite of our different personalities, but Brody and I had always understood that our friendship was because of our differences. We balanced each other well.

"I'm surprised to see you up at all," I replied, "what with all the scotch you must be drinking. Sampling the wares?"

"Lads."

"Sorry, Da."

We said it together, our accents thickening in response to Da's. Brody had lost a bit more of it than I had, but whenever we were around another Scot, it was as if we'd never left.

I turned my attention from Brody to my other two siblings at the table. Eoin had been home for nearly four months, but I'd only seen him the once when we'd had a welcome home party for him. The scar that ran down his left cheek from his temple to just under his mouth had been ragged and pink then. Now, it looked smoother, lighter. The other scars he'd received while overseas were hidden under his clothes. One day, all of them might fade until they were barely noticeable.

The shadowed, haunted look in Eoin's usually vivid green eyes, however, might never heal.

"How have you been?"

Eoin shrugged, and out of the corner of my eye, I caught our parents exchanging concerned looks. He'd always been the quiet, brooding one, sullen, actually, but the army had changed him. Now that he'd been discharged, we were all worried that the troubled Eoin would come back.

I didn't press the question. I loved my brother and I hated what had happened to him, but I had my own problems to deal with at the moment.

"Paris, it's good to see you."

At twenty-eight, Paris and Eoin were a little under four months apart in age, with Paris being the elder of the two by seven months. How their birthdays fell meant they were in the same class at school, but it had taken kids a while to realize that they were siblings since Theresa's kids from her first marriage had kept their late father's last name – Carideo. Oddly enough, both names basically meant the same thing: *grace*.

"You too, Alec." She smiled at me. "And it's even better to see Evanne." She winked at her niece, who giggled.

"Did you get to be Indiana Jones?" Evanne asked.

I looked at my sister with a raised eyebrow. "Now,

where would she be getting the idea that you're Indiana Jones?"

"I'm surprised that you know who that is, Alec," Paris countered. "When was the last time you actually watched a movie?"

"We watched the dragon movies together," Evanne announced. "All three of them."

Paris looked at me, her dark eyes warm. "He's a good dad."

"The best."

My daughter's matter-of-fact agreement made me smile. What had I done to deserve such a sweet and loyal child? The answer was absolutely nothing, and I still hadn't figured out how she'd ended up so amazing. It certainly didn't come from me, and while Keli wasn't a horrible woman, she wasn't even close to the amazing person our daughter was becoming.

"Grandma said we could go shopping today."

"I said we would go if it was okay with your father," Theresa corrected gently. "He might have something for you to do today."

"I don't," I said. "I think a day out would be just the thing."

"Yay!" Evanne threw her hands in the air. "Can we go to the waterfalls?"

I gave Theresa a questioning look.

"Blackhawk Plaza in Danville."

A flicker of memory brought the image of the shopping plaza, complete with waterfalls. Theresa had taken Evanne there to go Christmas shopping last winter, and Evanne had gone on and on about how much she loved the plaza and how pretty everything had been.

"I think that's a great idea," Theresa said to Evanne. "What if Aunt Paris came with us?"

Evanne immediately jumped out of her chair and ran around the table to Paris, begging her to come with them.

"She looks like she's doing okay," Brody pitched his voice low, his normally easy-going expression shifting to something far more serious. "Da told me what happened."

"I wish I actually knew what happened," I said honestly. "Either no one knows what happened, or no one's talking. Rumors are everywhere, but I'm trying to ignore them."

"But she didn't see anything?"

I shook my head.

The relief on Brody's face reflected just how much he loved his niece. Everyone in my family did. It didn't matter if we were related by blood or by law, and it didn't matter how difficult it had been for us to become accustomed to being a family. It's what we were.

"While the lasses are off together, perhaps you lads will join me for a round of golf?" Da popped the last piece of sausage into his mouth.

"That depends," Brody said with a grin. "Are you going to lecture everyone about how Americans have ruined a good Scottish game?"

The look Da gave my brother was stern, but that was just how he was. Ma had always said I was just like him. The older I got, the more I realized that she'd been right. If Theresa thought the same, she'd never mentioned it. She and I'd had a rocky start, but we'd eventually found our footing with each other. We just weren't close.

Except she'd been the first person I'd called when Keli had dropped off Evanne and left for Italy. And she'd come immediately.

Maybe I still needed to try a wee bit harder with her.

"Aye, all right. I'll behave myself," Da promised.

It looked like we were going golfing.

I HAD NOT MISSED San Ramon temperatures, something of which I was reminded as my brothers and I followed Da on the golf course. At least Evanne was getting a great day to go shopping at the plaza. Being in and out of air-conditioned stores on a sunny, mid-eighties day would be just what she needed to get her mind off what had happened at school.

It wouldn't be as easy for me.

Usually, I would've buried myself in work, but I wasn't quite rude enough to lock myself in a room with my laptop. Perhaps Da would've understood. He'd built the business, after all. But I didn't want to be rude.

Spending the day like this, however, wasn't so bad. The Bridges Golf Course was absolutely beautiful, and it had been a long time since I'd spent this much time with my family. When Eoin had decided not to re-enlist after he'd been injured, we'd all come home to welcome him back, but I'd only stayed for the few hours.

I'd had a meeting to get back to.

Brody and I hung back as Da and Eoin walked ahead. Neither of them were saying much, but that wasn't anything new.

"How's Eoin doing?" I asked Brody quietly. "I know I've been caught up in everything with Evanne recently, but I should have been more involved after he got back."

Brody didn't quite manage to cover his surprise fast enough. Shame flooded me because I knew I deserved it. I loved my family, but I showed it by working hard to make MIRI even more successful. We all had shares in it. Still, I knew none of them expected me to spend as much time at work as I did. Convincing myself that it was how I cared for my family gave me the excuse I needed to close myself off from everyone.

I knew I had issues. This wasn't the time for introspection, though. What had happened, however, did make me more aware of some things I could change. The first thing on my list was to find out how Eoin was doing.

"I dinnae ken," Brody said after a minute. He cleared his throat. "You know how the lad is. Close-mouthed and all that. Can't get a word out of him."

I didn't like the sound of that.

"Is he going back to how he was?"

Brody shrugged. "With some luck, Paris might get him to talk. They've always been close."

"How long is she here?" I asked, shifting the conversation. Brody was right. If anyone could get Eoin to talk, it would be Paris.

"She's leaving again this weekend. Doing some lecture work."

We stopped at the next hole and watched as Da teed up.

"You never told me how things went with the lass. The one from the massage parlor."

I glanced toward Eoin and Da to make sure neither of them heard. At the moment, Brody was the only one who knew about the incident, and I intended to keep it that way. It had been an uncharacteristic lack of judgment. One I was grateful for as I enjoyed Lumen's company, but not one I wished to share. If I spoke to the rest of my family about it, I'd be sure to give a vaguer explanation.

"She's Evanne's teacher." When Brody's eyes widened, I allowed myself a small smile. "My life has been a wee bit strange the past few weeks..."

SIX

LUMEN

I MUST'VE BEEN MORE TIRED THAN I'D THOUGHT because I didn't wake up Tuesday morning until my phone rang, jarring me out of a deep sleep. I fumbled for it, my foggy brain trying to figure out why I was still in bed rather than at work.

"Hello?" Damn, my voice sounded rough.

"Lumen?"

For a moment, I didn't recognize the male voice on the other end, but then he continued, and I wished I hadn't picked up my phone at all.

"It's Vice Principal Harvey here."

I silently cursed my foul luck. "Mr. Harvey, good morning. Is something wrong?"

"Nothing new, no. Did I catch you at a bad time? Still in bed?"

If he asked what I was wearing, no power on earth would keep me from telling him exactly what I thought of him. "No, not a bad time. How can I help you?"

"Principal McKenna tasked me with personally contacting all faculty members regarding yesterday's incident."

I could almost see the pompous windbag puffing himself up like this was some sacred duty he'd been entrusted instead of him just doing his job.

My tolerance for people wasn't generally high right after I woke up to begin with, and being woken up by one of my least favorite people in the world hadn't made it any better. Only a lifetime of learning restraint kept me cordial.

"Most importantly, the school will remain closed through the week to ensure that all of our students and faculty have the time to process what happened and their feelings toward it. We'll have counselors available at the school who specialize in this type of thing."

I had to admit, I was more than a little surprised that they'd decided to take the entire week. Sadly, school shootings had become commonplace enough that, most of the time, even in cases where there had been fatalities, schools only took a day or two before being back in session. I really hoped that didn't mean things had been worse yesterday than what they'd seemed.

"Do we know what happened?" I asked, dreading the answer while at the same time needing to know. The sleep fog had finally cleared, and I was no longer in a rush to get him off the phone.

"The official investigation isn't closed yet," Harvey said, "but the word is that it was an accident."

"An accident?" I echoed. I pushed myself up until I was sitting. Some kid had accidentally shot up a school?

"Apparently, one of the junior high students had brought his father's gun to school to show his friends before lunch. He started playing with it, pretending to target practice or something along those lines. He claims that he didn't know it was loaded."

I'd heard more than one gunshot so there had to be more to the story.

Harvey continued, "He told the police that he hadn't wanted to look like a wimp to his friends so when the first shot startled him, he decided to pretend he'd done it on purpose. He aimed at a poster on the wall and shot a couple more times intentionally. One of those shots ricocheted, and the substitute for Mr. Clark was injured. They're still trying to determine if it was shrapnel or the bullet itself, but either way, he just needed a few stitches, and it probably won't even scar."

Relief flooded through me. I hadn't wanted to consider the possibility that someone had been seriously injured, and it was being kept quiet, but the thought had been there, hovering in the back of my mind. Any injury wasn't good, and the emotional effect on the other students and the faculty wasn't anything to dismiss lightly, but it could have been so much worse.

"The young man who brought the gun in has been suspended, but Principal McKenna and I will be speaking with his family to determine if a two-week suspension is a harsh enough punishment for the severity of the crime. Since it wasn't deliberate, the police are going to work with us and the parents to come to the best solution for all involved."

I didn't need to have grown up in a privileged world to know what all of that meant. In fact, *not* growing up that way had taught me all too well how things like this went.

The kid who'd brought the gun to school had parents who were powerful and wealthy enough to cause problems should the situation not be handled in a way they liked. Since other students also came from influential families, the school couldn't completely sweep things under the rug, but they had to find the balance that would satisfy everyone. If the substitute who'd been injured decided to press charges, then there'd probably be a payout of some kind, and the shooter might not even get a legal slap on the wrist.

I was suddenly glad that these weren't the sort of decisions I had to be involved in making. When school began again on Monday, all I'd have to worry about was my class, and the higher ups could deal with the politics of the situation.

"Is there anything Principal McKenna wants the teachers doing this week?" I asked.

"We'll be meeting thirty minutes earlier than usual on Monday morning, and we can address any concerns we might have then. But you're welcome to call me anytime if you have anything you need to talk about."

I stifled a sigh but allowed a frown. Of course he was going to go there. He'd been flirting with me from moment one...if what he was doing could even be considered flirting. It probably would've been more accurate to call it harassment, but I put up with it because the alternative could get me fired. He hadn't quite crossed the line, but he did enjoy dancing close to it.

"I'm fine, thank you." I looked at my phone's screen. "Listen, I have an appointment I need to get ready for, so if there's nothing else..."

I let the sentence trail off and hoped he'd take the not-so-subtle hint.

Miracles of miracles, he did.

"I'll let you go then, but that offer is always open.

And if you don't want to talk on the phone, we can always go out to eat, then come back to my place. Or your place."

I rubbed my forehead. "All right, thank you. I'll keep that in mind."

Like hell was *that* ever going to happen, but it at least allowed me to end the call.

I hadn't lied when I'd said that I had an appointment, but it wasn't until this afternoon, so I had plenty of time to get ready, and I wouldn't even have to rush. But I did have something I had to do first.

As I opened my messages, I reminded myself that I wasn't texting Alec for personal reasons. I was respecting the fact that he'd said he'd contact me when they were back. But I did need to make sure that he knew the true story, if only so he could reassure Evanne.

Okay, maybe that was just an excuse, but I wasn't going to let it become personal.

If you haven't heard yet, school will be out for the rest of the week. We'll resume on Monday. It seems the incident was an accident, not a malicious attack. Once the investigation is officially closed, a statement will be released.

I paused, then added something that was a little personal.

I hope you and Evanne reached your parents safely.

After I sent it, I spent a moment looking at my phone, but then purposefully put it aside. I wasn't going to wait for him to get back to me. He was with his family. Besides, I had things to do too.

SEVEN

LUMEN

PART OF BEING IN THE FOSTER SYSTEM WAS DEALING with caseworkers, and while I wasn't technically *working* in or for the system, I still sometimes met the social workers when I was around the group home. Josalyn Brodie hadn't been one of those, so when I stepped into the lobby of the Department of Child and Family Services, I wasn't sure who I was looking for or where I was going. Fortunately, one caseworker I did know spotted me right away.

"Lumen Browne." Donna Bedford beamed as she came toward me. Her hug was both familiar and welcome, and a single inhalation of apple-scented body wash took me right back to being thirteen when my first caseworker had retired, and I'd been passed off to Donna. Henry had been okay. Donna was better.

"Hey, Donna."

"I've heard you've been working with some of the kids at Brie Richards' place."

I nodded. "I have. Actually, that's why I'm here. One of her girls, Soleil Artz, reached out to me yesterday, but then changed her mind about telling me whatever was troubling her. I want to talk to her caseworker and see if I can get some ideas about how to get through to her or what she might have to say."

"Who is it?"

"Josalyn Brodie."

"She's a good woman," Donna said. "Tough and a little jaded, but she still cares. C'mon. I'll take you to her."

I followed Donna through the cubicles to one closer to the back.

"Josalyn." Donna rapped her knuckles on the divider. "This is Lumen Browne. She talked to you about one of your kids."

Josalyn looked like she was in her late forties, her jet-black hair in braids that nearly went to her waist. Her dark eyes were intelligent and stern, the sort of person who took her job seriously.

"Ms. Brodie." I held out a hand.

"Don't leave without saying goodbye," Donna said as she walked away.

"I won't," I promised as Josalyn shook my hand. "Thank you for seeing me."

"Please, sit."

I did as she asked. "I know it's unorthodox, talking to a...well, to someone who doesn't officially work in the foster system. I appreciate it."

"I wasn't going to," she admitted, "but I know Soleil's had some problems, and Brie says that you're one of the few people who's been getting through to her."

"I'm trying," I said. "Did Brie tell you who I am? I mean, how we know each other?"

"She mentioned you were one of her kids, but that was about it. I didn't look up your file."

I wouldn't have blamed her if she'd pulled up my file just to be sure I didn't have any red flags in my background, but it didn't surprise me that she didn't bend or break rules without great consideration.

"Brie's house was the last place I ended up," I said. "I went into the system when I was seven. My parents signed away their rights, and I never saw them again."

One good thing about telling my story to people who worked in the system was that, while some expressed empathy, none of them pitied me, especially since I knew my story wasn't even close to as bad as most others.

"Yesterday, Soleil called me while I was at work." This was verging on breaking Soleil's trust, but I needed to know more, and to learn that, I had to convince Josalyn that I could be trusted. "Then she came to see me, but I had a lot going on, and by the time we were able to talk, she no longer wanted to."

The last thing I needed was to get Soleil in trouble for skipping school, but it was a risk I felt like I needed to take. Josalyn studied me, and I let her, knowing she needed time to make her decision. When she nodded, a bit of the tension in me released.

"Soleil's been in and out of the system since birth. Her mom's an alcoholic, and there's never been a father in the picture. A year ago, Soleil's mom went to prison for hitting someone while driving drunk. The person wasn't hurt too badly, but it was a third offense, so she ended up getting a longer sentence than she might have otherwise."

I nodded. "Yeah, that'd make most people cynical."

"She's also had four different caseworkers. The first retired. The second got married and moved away. The one before me was fired for taking bribes to look the other way in a trafficking ring that ran through one of the group homes."

"Shit." Probably not the best thing to say, but it seemed appropriate. "I remember reading about that. The asshole social worker was Soleil's?" A horrible thought occurred to me. "She wasn't..." I didn't have the heart to finish the sentence.

Josalyn shook her head. "The home she was with when that happened was actually a good one. She probably would've stayed there if the older couple hadn't run into some health problems. The woman had a heart attack, the man a stroke. Neither one of them was capable of caring for a head-strong, rebellious ten-year-old."

My heart broke for the girl I barely knew. I hadn't known the same depth of pain and hurt that she had, but I hoped now that I understood her a bit better, I could reach her.

"Thank you," I said. "It helps, knowing her history. Can you think of anything that's happening now that I should know about?"

Josalyn took the time to think about it before shaking her head. "I can't think of anything specific. I'm not her confidant, though. I'm sure there's a lot I don't know." She leaned forward. "And I'm hoping you'll be able to help her through it."

EIGHT

ALEC

When Keli and I had set up our custody arrangement, I'd been certain that the best thing for our daughter would be to have Keli be the primary caregiver and me to be the financial support. I had loved my daughter from the moment I'd learned about her – after I'd gotten over the shock – and I'd honestly believed that was in her best interest to keep her time with me to short periods that I couldn't fuck up. Since she'd turned out to be such an amazing person, I thought that meant I'd made the right choice, no matter how much I wished I could've made a family for her.

What I'd never thought of was how much of her life I'd missed.

Not the things like her first steps or her first word. Even if Keli and I had been married, I probably would have missed them due to work and seen them on video just as I had, anyway.

No, it was the small things I hadn't even known to miss. Like sitting on the couch while she showed me every single thing that she and Theresa and Paris had bought today. And it wasn't a simple show and tell where she held up the clothing. She insisted on modeling everything.

If someone had told me two months ago that I would spend three hours watching Evanne put on a fashion show and listening to her explain to me how the dinosaur model Paris had bought would help when she became a vet, I would've told them that was insane. But sitting here with my family, laughing more than I'd laughed with them in a long time, it made me realize that I had sold myself short.

"Want me to help you start putting that together?" Paris asked Evanne after the fashion show was done.

I wondered which of the two of them was actually more excited about the dinosaur and smiled when they moved over to the low table Theresa had put in the den specifically for these sorts of projects. I knew she and Da were always hoping to have more opportunities to use it.

At the moment, however, they'd stepped out to take some food to a friend of theirs who'd recently fallen and broken her leg. Brody had left the golf course, saying he had a new batch of scotch to test. I was glad Paris had stayed. Evanne didn't get to spend nearly enough time with her aunts and uncles, which was my fault, I knew. At least that was something I could begin to rectify now that Evanne was with me full-time.

"I have to ask." I kept watching Evanne even as I spoke to Eoin. "How are you not going mad here, brother?"

Eoin shrugged. "They give me my space."

I didn't bother pressing for details. He wouldn't give them. My little brother was one of the few people in the family who talked even less than I did. Except for when he'd been in the army. Then, he'd loved telling stories about the things he and his friends would do. Not the serious things like the missions they went on, but the pranks they would pull on each other, that sort of thing. Now, none of us wanted to ask about what happened those last few weeks.

"Have you heard from Keli?" he asked, surprising me with the question.

"I haven't," I said. "I called to let her know about the shooting at the school, but she didn't answer. I left a voicemail letting her know Evanne was all right and that we'd be here."

I suddenly remembered that I hadn't checked my phone in a few hours, an occurrence that hadn't happened in a very long time. When I pulled it out, I saw I had nothing from Keli, but I had received a text from Lumen. I read through it as Eoin waited and then pressed my voice-to-text option to reply.

"Thank you for the update. We got in last night without any problems."

After sending it off, I caught Eoin giving me a curious look.

"That didn't sound like a response to Keli."

"It wasn't," I said shortly. When he raised an eyebrow, I blew out a long breath. "If you must know, it was an update from Evanne's school. They're closed the rest of the week, and it seems that the incident was an accident of some kind."

"Does that mean we're staying for the week?" Evanne asked. "Because if I can't go to school, I'd rather be here."

"You don't have any friends you want to play with?" Paris asked.

Evanne shrugged. "I have a friend named Skylar, but I don't want to have a play date with him. I don't like his mom."

"Evanne," I chided. "You cannae say things like that, *mo chride.*"

"Why not?" she asked. "I heard her tell Skylar that

Ms. Browne was trailer trash, and even though I don't know what that means, I know it isn't nice."

A flare of anger went through me, and my hands curled into fists before I'd even realized I'd done it. I'd met Skylar's mother once when I'd picked up Evanne, and I wished I could have told my daughter that she'd misunderstood what that foul woman had said, but it didn't surprise me in the least.

"You're right," Eoin spoke after a beat of tense silence. "That's not a nice thing to call someone."

"I didn't think so," she said. "Skylar was upset about it too, but she's his mom so he can't tell her what not to say. She's not my mom, though, so if she says it again, I'm going to tell her it's mean."

For a moment, I allowed myself to entertain the vision of Evanne having that conversation, but it wasn't something I could support for several reasons, not the least of which was that I doubted Mrs. Crenshaw would even hesitate to be rude to my daughter, and that would just start a whole pile of shite.

"If she says it again, I want you to tell me," I said. "I'll take care of it."

"Good." Evanne smiled brightly. "You should stand up for people you care about, like Ms. Browne."

Eoin glanced at me. "Who is this Ms. Browne?"

"Evanne's teacher," I answered automatically.

"Daddy calls her Lumen, and sometimes I do too, but not when I'm at school."

Heat flooded my face. I now had both of my siblings looking at me with questions in their eyes. I didn't know how to respond to Evanne's statement. It was true, so I couldn't have said she was wrong or pretending or anything like that, not even if she hadn't been listening too. But I wasn't sure if I was ready to tell my family that I was sort of seeing Evanne's teacher. If that was what we were doing. I still didn't know.

Aye, I'd decided I wanted more than a single night of fun with her, and I'd given her a house key, but we'd had no discussion about what any of that meant. Wouldn't the gentlemanly thing to do, the right thing to do, be to talk to her before I started using labels?

"Lumen..." I cleared my throat. "Ms. Browne has been helping Evanne adjust to the new school and the new...circumstances." All of that was true. "She's a kind lass, and Evanne is quite taken with her."

Paris seemed to accept my explanation and went back to helping Evanne with the dinosaur kit. Eoin didn't press the issue, but the skepticism in his eyes said he hadn't been completely taken in. He suspected there was more to the story than I was saying.

He was right.

Our parents knew about Lumen. Well, I'd talked to

Da about her, and he and Theresa kept no secrets between them, which meant she knew too. Da had been the one I'd gone to when I'd needed advice, and a part of me wanted to go to him again with this. What held me back was that I hadn't brought Evanne here for me to deal with my romantic life. We were here for her, to keep her mind off what had happened and to process what she couldn't forget.

Perhaps if I kept telling myself that shite lie, I might eventually believe it.

For someone who considered himself a man of integrity, I was messing about with the truth an awful lot.

NINE

LUMEN

Josalyn had given me plenty to think about, and I knew I wasn't going to figure it all out at once, so when I got back home, I declined Mai's offer to watch a movie with her and her boyfriend, saying I'd head to my room after dinner to get ahead on some work. I liked Hob well enough, and Mai was the closest thing to family that I'd ever had, but I wasn't in the mood for company tonight. I had too much going on in my head.

Besides, with Hob's crazy work schedule, he and Mai didn't get as much alone time as I knew they both would've liked. He was a third-year resident working toward becoming a pediatrician, and just a generally good man. The two of them had been together for a while now, and I wouldn't be surprised if a ring was in the near future.

I wished all the best for them.

And I wasn't jealous at all.

I allowed myself a small smile as I bid them good-night and settled in my room. It wasn't very big, but at least it was all mine. I'd shared a room most of my life, and while I knew it'd been that way for a lot of kids, even one who'd grown up with real families, it didn't make me appreciate having a room to myself any less.

I sat on my bed and opened my lesson plan book, laying it flat on the bedspread. I liked to write out a basic overview for each quarter, but that often meant I had to adapt things as the days went by. I supposed by the time I'd been doing this for a few years, I'd be tired of working that far ahead and having to tweak things. Right now, however, I intended to stick with what I'd been doing so far.

I'd gotten through my early lessons yesterday the way I'd planned, but I'd be a full week behind in my afternoon classes. I'd need to adapt if I wanted to stay on track. With that thought in mind, I took out a notebook and began copying down the things that were absolutely necessary and took out the extra things I'd put in for filler, exactly for instances like this. It was nice to have fun activities that supplemented the lessons, but if I needed the time, they were easy to take out.

I'd made my way through half of next week when

my phone rang. I felt the smile spread from ear to ear when Alec's name popped up on my screen. I told myself not to sound too eager and waited until after the second ring before I answered it.

"Hello there, Mr. McCrae." I closed my eyes and slapped a hand to my forehead. I'd intended to say something light and flirty, but I was fairly certain that I'd only sounded creepy.

"Ms. Browne." The hint of humor in his voice chased away my mortification. "It's good to hear your voice."

"And yours." I pushed my things aside and stretched my legs out to get more comfortable. I deserved a break anyhow. "How's Evanne doing?"

"She's enjoying herself. Her grandma and aunt took her shopping."

"And what about yesterday?" I asked, even though I hated bringing that horrible day back to life. "How's she doing with that?"

"She doesn't know anything," he said. "I'll tell her what happened when the news is released, but I'm going to keep it matter-of-fact. I don't want her to be scared to go to school."

"I'm glad she didn't hear or see anything," I said.

"What about you?" His voice dropped an octave lower. "How are you doing with it?"

"I'm all right," I said honestly. "Once I heard what'd really happened, it made a difference. I've mostly been worried about the kids."

An awkward silence stretched between us for several seconds before he spoke again.

"What did you do today?"

I didn't blame him for not wanting to discuss anything else serious. Not over the phone. We needed to keep things light.

Which meant curtailing what I'd done rather than telling him about what was going on with Soleil. That was okay, though. I was invested in his daughter, so of course, I wanted to know how she was doing. Alec didn't know Soleil.

"After I texted you, I ran some errands. Nothing exciting."

"And what are you doing right now?"

"Fixing my lesson plans for next week."

"That's true, you would need to adapt when there's a change in schedule."

"That's why teachers both love and hate snow days," I joked. "What about you? What are you doing right now?"

"Talking to you."

I rolled my eyes even though he couldn't see me. "I'm surprised you're not using this time to work."

"To be honest, lass," he said with a chuckle, "I am too."

Warmth flooded me. He'd chosen talking to me over work. "Are you finally admitting you might need time to relax?"

"Maybe..." he said slowly.

"You're forgetting," I said, my voice deepening unconsciously, "that I know just how tense you get."

Memories came flooding back. The way he'd felt under my hands, hard muscle, and warm skin. The scent of sandalwood and him – a scent that I had craved ever since. My first glimpse of that magnificent body stretched out on my table. The way his erection, hidden beneath an almost-too-small towel, had caused my pussy to throb even before I knew what it felt like to have him inside me.

"That's right, lass." His voice deepened in turn, his accent thickening with each word. "You do. And you ken how to fix it better than anyone."

I shivered, muscles low in my belly tightening. "I really hope you're not just talking about my massage technique."

"As enjoyable as that was, no, it's not what I'm referencing." After a long pause, he asked, "Are you alone?"

"Yeah, I'm in my room." I finished the sentence before understanding hit me.

Oh.

"What are you wearing?"

A bolt of lust went through me. "Pajamas."

"More."

I couldn't believe I was about to do this. And that I was wearing probably the unsexyist thing ever. "A tank top that says *I like big books* on it and a pair of yoga pants."

He chuckled, and it was easily the sexiest fucking thing I'd ever heard. "I'll be wanting you to wear those sometime."

"So you can take them off me?"

Another laugh. "No, lass. I'd like to fuck you in them. Bend you over and pull those down just far enough for me to be able to slide inside you."

I let out a breath and settled into a more comfortable position. It appeared we were going to do this.

"It'd be easy," I teased, "since I'm not wearing any underwear."

Alec muttered a curse. "Yer killin' me, Lumen."

"Am I?" I cupped one of my breasts over my tank top. "Then I suppose I shouldn't tell you that my nipples are getting hard?"

Heat flooded my face, half from embarrassment, but the other half was from arousal. This was so not like me.

But I'd done a lot of things with Alec that I'd never done before.

And I'd liked them all.

"Shite, Lumen. You say something like that, and we're so far apart?" He almost sounded like he was in pain...but the sort of pain that came with being too turned on.

"Is your hand broken?"

"Lumen," he growled the warning.

"My hand's not broken," I teased. "And right now, it's going under the waistband of my pants."

My skin was already overheated, and my fingers found me wet. I closed my eyes and pretended he was the one touching me. I hadn't really done much of this before, but I remembered what his hands felt like, and I had a pretty good idea of what I was doing.

"How wet are you?" he asked.

"Soaked."

He groaned. "I'm touching myself now, wishing it was you."

"I like the sound of that." My fingers skimmed over my clit, and sparks of pleasure tingled across my nerves. "Moving my hand up and down your thick cock."

"While my fingers slide inside you."

I sighed as I pushed two fingers inside me. A shudder went through me at the minor stretch. I could've used all four fingers, and they wouldn't have been as thick as Alec's cock.

"Move my hand up and down, faster, squeeze you tighter." I pressed the heel of my hand against my clit, and sparks danced behind my eyelids.

"Run my tongue down your cleft, taste that sweet cunt."

His accent was so thick, I could barely understand what he was saying, but it didn't matter. Just the sound of his voice got me hot.

"Take you in my mouth as deep as I can. Suck you until you explode in my mouth."

"Fuck, *mo nighean*."

My girl, my lass. I was close, going from zero to a hundred in less time than should have been possible.

"*Mhurinn*."

I recognized that one too. *My darling*.

The pressure inside me built, heat from his words and pleasure from my hands. I bit my bottom lip to keep myself quiet, soft whimpers and moans escaping despite it. Alec's breathing was harsh, mingling with the sound of flesh moving against flesh, and I could picture how he must've looked. Thick cock in hand. Muscles tight. Expression filled with the sort of tension that could only find relief in orgasm.

"I want to be inside you."

His words made me shiver, made me clench around my fingers. "I want that too."

"Tell me, lass. Tell me what you want."

My breathing hitched at the sound of pure need in those words. "I want to hear you come. Hear you say my name and know that you're thinking of me, remembering what it feels like when we're together."

I couldn't believe I was telling him this, sharing things I only ever thought...and still holding back the one thing I couldn't acknowledge, not even to myself.

It had to be *want* and not *need*. I couldn't *need* him. Not in any way that really mattered.

"Are you close, *mo nighean*?"

"Yes." I repeated the affirmation. "Yes."

My hips moved against my hand, and pleasure tore through me, arcing through my body like lightning. All heat and power and light. Hundreds of miles away, Alec followed me, calling out my name. In that moment, the space between us disappeared, and we were together in that way that obliterated all obstacles and made me feel like anything was possible.

TEN
ALEC

FOR ME, SEX HAD ALWAYS BEEN AN ENJOYABLE WAY to blow off steam, a place to be in control, but never an impulse I felt I needed a certain number of times in a specific timeframe. As such, I'd only indulged when the urge struck, and my schedule allowed for it.

Then I'd met Lumen.

Of all the sexual things I'd done in my life, I'd never had phone sex until last night. In the past, if I'd wanted physical release but hadn't wanted to bother finding a partner, I would take care of it myself, no one else needed. Last night, however, I'd wanted to talk to Lumen, and it had turned into something sexual.

"Get yer head outta yer arse, McCrae," I muttered to myself as I shook my head.

ER

It was the middle of the week, and things had been piling up at work since I'd taken that abrupt leave Monday afternoon. I hadn't done more than check in yesterday, which meant I'd spent all of this morning simply catching up on email. Fortunately, I had a good reputation, which meant once I'd explained to my clients that there'd been an incident at my daughter's school, no one would hold my brief absence against me.

At least, they wouldn't be vocal about it. No one wanted to be the person known for criticizing a man whose child had been present during a shooting.

I finished the email I'd been writing and sent it off. That had been the last one...except I'd gotten responses to the first five I sent out. I sighed and went back to the top. When had this become so tedious? Hadn't I enjoyed my work?

Try as I might, I couldn't quite remember anything similar to joy or even happiness. Perhaps some pride and satisfaction when I was able to show Da how well I'd done with the company he'd created, but certainly no enjoyment.

Not that I felt as if I had the right to complain about any of it. I was worth billions, and the work we did was good. Both the company and I personally contributed astronomical sums to various charities. We made the world better.

78

Shouldn't that have been enough?

Now that I had Evanne in my life, keeping me from being entirely consumed by my job, I wondered what I'd been doing all these years, missing out on being an integral part of my daughter's life when I could have easily adjusted my time at work to be with her more.

Thoughts like that made it difficult to concentrate, and I was grateful for the interruption when Theresa knocked on the study door.

"Keli's here."

It took a moment for the words to process, and still, I needed to hear them again. "What?"

"Keli is here." Theresa's expression was blank, but I knew she'd never approved of my ex. The way she'd left Evanne with me hadn't helped matters much. "She's in the front room."

Assuming that this would take a good portion of the rest of my day, I closed everything down, taking the extra couple minutes to run through various possible reasons for her sudden appearance, not the least of which was that she'd decided that I wasn't suited to be a full-time parent. The problem was, I hadn't as of yet decided if I agreed with that assessment or not.

I was still several feet from the front room when I heard Evanne laughing. My stomach clenched. For the most part, Keli and I hadn't butted heads when it came to our daughter, and the big reason for that on my part had been me not wanting to put Evanne in the middle of something that wasn't her fault or her responsibility. She loved her mom, and I'd have to have been a right bastard to take that away from her simply because Keli and I weren't suited for each other.

"Good afternoon," I said as I stepped into the room.

Keli was seated on the floor next to Evanne, showing her something that I assumed was a present from Italy. When she looked up at me, I was struck again at how much Evanne looked like a perfect combination of us two. Keli's curls were ebony to Evanne's dark brown, eyes teal rather than blue, the differences owing to my blond hair and blue eyes. Evanne's features were the same, a little of me and a little of Keli. The nose that was mine had come from my own mother, and that was bittersweet. Ma would have loved knowing her grand-daughter.

"Always so formal, Alec," Keli said with a smile.

I waited for her to tell me why she was here, but when she didn't, I sat next to Evanne on the floor. Ignoring Keli's surprised expression, I took a good look at my daughter, searching her face for any negative emotion. I'd only been partially honest with Evanne when it came to why her mother had left, not lying outright, but hiding the full truth. I'd simply said that Keli had wanted to go somewhere with her boyfriend, and Evanne needed to go to school here. I refused to cause Evanne the hurt that the full truth would bring, but I wasn't certain Keli had the same compunction.

"Look what Mommy brought me." Evanne held up a doll, the expression on her face one of pure delight. "She said it was for being so brave at school."

I glanced at Keli for only a second before turning my attention back to Evanne. "It's lovely, *mo chride.*"

"Was it difficult to get a last-minute flight?" Theresa asked with a smile. "You must have been on the phone all day and night trying to get here."

I heard a cough from the far side of the room where Paris was sitting and knew she was trying to mask a laugh. My stepmother was generally sweet and soft-spoken, but when it came to the people she loved, she was one of the fiercest women I knew. She never responded by yelling or making threats. No, she was the sort of woman who eviscerated people with words.

Keli's smile tightened. "I flew standby, so I didn't have to use my phone. The roaming charges in Italy are horrendous. It cost me just to listen to the voicemail Alec left. Better to use my phone as little as possible rather than run up an astronomical bill."

My gut said she wanted me to offer to pay her phone bill whenever she wanted to use her phone while in Italy, but that wasn't going to happen. Her new boyfriend was the one who hadn't wanted Evanne, and she'd chosen to be with him. Let her get the money from him. I'd been more than generous over the last eight years, but I'd done it for my daughter. Not for Keli.

"I'm surprised no one offered to let you use their phone, considering the reason you were coming home."

Da put his hand on Theresa's arm.

Keli's eyes narrowed for a moment before she fixed a neutral expression on her face. "Calls made from Italian phones would've ended up with long-distance charges, and I wouldn't ask anyone to pay that."

"Did you ride one of the boats?" Evanne's question reminded all of us that no matter the reasons for our animosity toward each other, we had one much larger reason to keep things civil.

"What boats, sweetie?" Keli asked as she smoothed down Evanne's curls.

"The ones that go through the streets because they're flooded. I asked Ms. Browne to help me find pictures from Italy, and one of them had people in boats."

A sliver of panic poked up its head. The last thing

Keli needed to know about was my relationship with Lumen. I wasn't worried about her being jealous of me, but rather her jealousy over how much Evanne admired Lumen. As just a teacher, it wouldn't be quite so threatening.

"Ms. Browne?"

"My teacher."

It was all I could do not to cross my fingers or mutter a prayer that Evanne wouldn't go any further with that thought.

"How long are you back?" I asked.

Evanne's head shot up. "You're leaving again?"

"No, sweetie." Keli's voice had a condescending tone I didn't like. "Mommy's going to be here as long as you need her."

The hope on Evanne's face broke my heart. If Keli left again with no warning, it'd devastate our daughter. If Keli decided to stay, it might mean that she would want primary custody back, and the thought of that didn't sit well with me, especially since that would mean I'd have to find out if Evanne wanted to stay with me...or go back to Keli.

"Our flight is Saturday morning," I said. "You're welcome to come back with us...if you're coming back to Seattle."

"I think I'll do that."

I'd done it for Evanne, to show her that, no matter the difficulties Keli and I had, I wasn't going to keep her mother from her. Maybe I wasn't doing it for the right reasons, wanting her to see that I was being the bigger person, but it was still the right choice to make.

"Well, Keli, it was nice of you to stop by and bring Evanne such a pretty gift." Theresa gave Keli one of those smiles that looked nice on the surface, but underneath held nothing but contempt. "Now, if you'll excuse us, I promised Evanne that we'd make tacos for dinner. From scratch, so we have a lot to do."

Keli stood, and I tensed, anticipating an argument. The short amount of time Keli and I had been together had been long enough for my entire family and her to figure out that they loathed each other. Since we'd split up, they hadn't seen each other, but my family's disdain of Keli had only grown.

"That sounds like fun."

From the startled look on Theresa's face, she hadn't expected that response any more than I had.

"You should stay and help!" Evanne grabbed Keli's hand. "Can she, Grandma?"

Theresa looked at me, and I shrugged. This wasn't my home or my decision to make.

"I'm sure your mother has more important things to do," Theresa said.

"I don't, actually." Keli squeezed Evanne's hand. "I already took my things to a hotel before I came here, so I'm free to spend as much time with you as you want."

Wonderful.

ELEVEN

LUMEN

After our little phone sex session, I thought I'd hear from Alec on a little more regular basis. Instead, I hadn't even gotten a text since that night, and it was now Friday evening. And no, I hadn't only been waiting for him to reach out first. When I hadn't heard from him by Wednesday afternoon, I'd texted him something I'd hoped was flirty, but now worried had sounded immature and flighty.

Hope you slept well last night. I know I did. Enjoy your time with your family, and tell Evanne I said hello.

I hadn't let my disappointment in the lack of contact take over my week, though. With an unexpected amount of extra time, I decided to do something good with it. For me, that meant spending the week at the group home, doing things with the kids, and trying to get through to Soleil.

Unfortunately, she'd maintained the same silence as she had when I'd taken her home on Monday. She still hadn't told me why she'd called me or why she'd come to the school. Knowing what I did now about her past, it would take a while to get through to her. Some of the other kids had their own walls up, but none of them had come to me the way Soleil had tried to, and I was determined not to make her regret it.

"Come see!" Diana Whitmore was thirteen and full of more energy than I could ever hope to have. "You can't leave until you see this!"

I let her drag me to the far side of the room. Mai had asked me to come to dinner with her family, and it was getting late, but I had enough time to see one last thing.

"What do you have for me, Sylvia?"

She giggled like she did every time I called her that. When I'd first found out this bouncy, happy child was obsessed with Sylvia Plath, I'd been surprised, but the more time I spent with her, the more I saw that the energy she expended was to keep at bay the darkness she held inside her. I didn't know what that darkness was about, but I hoped that she knew she could come to me if she ever wanted to talk about it.

"Look!" She pointed at a piece of paper hanging on

the bulletin board. "We had to write a poem for school, and I got an A!"

"That's great!" I gave her a hug. "I'm proud of you."

"Thank you." She beamed from ear to ear, bouncing on her toes. "My teacher said if I want to, I can turn it in for our school magazine."

"Good for you!" I might not have felt the same connection to Diana that I did to Soleil, but I would always support the positive things in these kids' lives.

"Thanks!"

After a few more seconds, something else caught her attention, and she bounced away. I gave a quick look around to see if Soleil was still hiding in the corner, but she'd disappeared. Brie probably knew where she was, but I wasn't going to go looking for her. It was a fine line to walk, letting a kid like her know I was there for her, but not being too pushy.

I caught Brie's attention and gestured toward the door. She nodded and smiled, then turned back to Kaitlyn and Kevin Parsons. From the somber expression on all three faces, I wondered if they were discussing Kaitlyn aging out of the system next year and how she hoped to be able to take custody of Kevin at that time. He was a little over a year younger than her, so even if she couldn't get custody of him, he wouldn't be in the system too long without her, but

Brie was worried that any time apart would be difficult for the two of them.

There had been times growing up where I'd thought it would have been nice to have had a sibling, but as I'd gotten older and realized how often siblings were split up in foster care, I'd become grateful to be an only child.

It wasn't until after I'd left the system that I'd found something like a family, and it was them I was on my way to see.

The bus was running late, which meant Mai was pacing by the time I let myself into the apartment. She pointed at me, glaring, and I held up both hands.

"Hey, I can't control the bus system."

"Right. Sure." Mai sighed. "But you get to explain that to my mom."

"Until I have a car, there's really not much of anything I can do about how prompt I am," I reminded her as I headed to my room. "Or how prompt I'm not, I guess."

"You know that, and I know that, and I'm pretty sure my mom *knows* that. Whether she'll accept that as a reason for us being late to dinner is another story."

"I'll explain it to her," I offered. "We both know that she likes me better."

Mai laughed. Lihua's preference for me over her daughter was something we'd been joking about since I'd answered Mai's ad for a roommate three years ago. She'd taken me home for a family dinner two days after I'd moved in, and it'd been there I'd met Mai's mother and siblings. Bao, Chang, Yun, Xue, Jie, and Ru, all of them immediately treating me like one of the family. I was another little sister to tease and protect, and it wasn't like anything I'd ever experienced before.

She and I couldn't have come from more different backgrounds if we'd tried, but every member of her family treated me as if I'd always been there with them. Working at the family massage parlor while getting my masters' degree in education had only solidified it. I still struggled to accept it at times, but I was getting better at it.

Fortunately for me, dressing for family dinner was easy. Dress pants and a casual long-sleeved blouse paired with sensible shoes. Unlike my roommate, I never needed to worry about whether or not an outfit was too revealing to be appropriate. It just wasn't my style. Lihua tended to be old-fashioned when it came to how her children dressed and behaved. To say that Mai didn't always meet those standards would be an understatement. Mai often flat-out defied them. Or she did something like tell her mom that she'd found a Chinese doctor to date but neglect to mention that Armani Hobson was only partially Chinese and mostly a mix of Haitian and

Caucasian, just to see her mom's reaction the first time Hob came to dinner.

"Is everyone coming tonight?" I asked as we walked out to the parking garage.

"I think Xue is sick, but everyone else should be there."

Xue was one of the middle daughters and was working on her doctorate in genetics. She was easily the smartest – and the quietest – of the bunch, which meant her absence wouldn't be as prominent as, say, oldest son Chang and his three boys.

The sheer size of the Jin family astounded me because it wasn't just siblings. Lihua's parents both lived with her, and their stories of growing up in China were always one of my favorite parts of dinner. They'd been in their fifties when they'd moved here with Lihua and loved to talk about the legacy their family had forged through the generations.

As far as I was aware, I didn't have grandparents or aunts or uncles. I certainly had no memory of them prior to being put in foster care, and there'd never been any mention of someone asking about me. Then again, if DCFS had found anyone, but they hadn't wanted me, it didn't necessarily mean that I would've been told.

"Did I tell you that Cal got early acceptance to

Yale?" Mai asked as we got into her car. "I thought Bao was going to rent a billboard to announce it."

As she pulled out of the garage and made the turn north, she kept up a steady stream of chatter, getting me up-to-date on what was going on with each of her siblings and their families. It took a few minutes for me to get my attention focused, but once I did, I made sure it stayed that way. I wasn't going to let Alec's silence dominate my thoughts. My life would not be ruled by the whim of a man.

Resolve in place, I smiled and asked Mai for details about her oldest niece's ballet recital.

TWELVE
ALEC

I'D NEVER DISLIKED SPENDING TIME WITH MY family, but I had always felt as if my time and attention would be better used elsewhere. Namely, at work.

I'd always known that I would take over MIRI one day, and quite without me realizing it, that had become my identity, even with my family. Instead of shifting that when Evanne was born, I'd worked even harder, seeing the family's legacy as passing down to her instead of seeing that I could have a different part in that legacy.

Becoming a full-time father without warning had shown me things about my life and myself that I wanted to change, namely how I wanted to be involved in Evanne's life. I hadn't realized until this week, however, just how much that change would affect my relationships with my family.

I hadn't completely ignored work this week, but I also hadn't let it consume me either. I'd spent time with Evanne, but also with everyone else too. While I'd enjoyed myself, I'd also finally realized how little I actually knew about what Eoin had gone through this past year.

Our parents hadn't talked to me about it, but being around them every day, I saw things that I either had missed before or that my parents had hidden. Little looks between the two of them, a hint of worry in their eyes, a tightening of their mouths. I might've thought that was a response to what had been going on with Evanne, but when I began paying attention, I caught that the pattern centered around my younger brother.

I knew he hadn't been sleeping well, so it was no surprise to me, as I went to the kitchen for a late-night snack, to find Eoin sitting at the table in near darkness. This house had always had small lights to keep the numerous inhabitants from tripping over or running into things as we had moved around at all hours growing up. It seemed that having a mostly empty nest hadn't changed much.

Eoin must've been in a mood to reminisce also, as all of his attention was focused on a picture in his hand. I only needed a glimpse to know what it was. I'd been the one to take it, after all. The day Eoin and his best friend, Leo McCormack, had left for basic training, they'd stood in front of this house, dressed in those khaki shorts and green shirts, and asked me to take their picture with the camera Da had bought Eoin for Christmas two years before.

I hadn't been close to Leo, but the pang of grief I felt was sincere.

"Can't sleep?" I kept my voice low in the hopes of not startling Eoin.

He shrugged, putting the picture face-down on the table and turning toward me. "It's still too quiet."

I doubted that was the entire story, but Eoin wasn't the sort to share anything simply because he was asked. If he wanted us to know something, he'd tell us. If he wished to keep to himself, he would do just that.

"Mom made shorties." He motioned to the plastic container next to the refrigerator.

"She's spoiling you," I said as I made for it.

The first New Year's Eve that the Carideo and McCrae families spent together, Theresa had surprised us with the traditional Scottish shortbread. Even as hurt and confused as I'd been by my father's sudden remarriage, my step-mother's willingness to go beyond her comfort zone to provide familiarity to kids who were far from home had spoken volumes to me. With the exception of a couple vague memories of our Ma, Theresa was the only mother Eoin had ever known.

One corner of Eoin's mouth ticked up. It wasn't a smile, and it lasted no more than a few seconds, but it was a change from the mask he'd been wearing since he'd come home.

"She made them for Evanne," he said. When I raised an eyebrow, I saw another flicker of humor. "And a bit for me."

I didn't know what he was going through, and I knew that me offering my help or a listening ear would be as awkward for him to hear as it would be for me to make, but he was in the right place to get whatever he needed, whenever he needed it. At the moment, I could offer him one thing, though.

"Shortie?"

"NOW, don't eat these all at once," Theresa told Evanne. "And make sure your dad eats a few of them. He pretends he doesn't like them, but I know he sneaks some whenever I have them around."

"They're wonderful," Keli said, taking the container from Evanne. "I'll carry them, sweetie." She looked back at the older woman. "Thank you, Theresa."

I could see it was on the tip of my stepmother's tongue to say something harsh. I cut in, "Aye, Mom, thank you."

Theresa smiled, as she always did when I called her *mom*. "You're welcome, as always."

"Before we leave," I said, "a reminder that Evanne's birthday is coming up, and I'll be having a party for her."

"Yay!" Evanne threw her hands up in the air.

"A birthday?" Da asked. "Dinnae you have one last year?"

"Grand-da!" Evanne gave him a disbelieving expression. "Everyone has a birthday every year!"

"Do they now?"

I enjoyed the banter between grandfather and granddaughter, both showing the same teasing sense of humor. I didn't notice Keli coming over to me until she took hold of my arm.

"We're thinking we'll rent a venue so Evanne can invite all of her little friends too."

All eyes turned to her, and my surprise at her statement kept me from shaking her hand off. Where had she gotten the idea that she would have anything to do with the planning of Evanne's birthday party? If she was still in Seattle, she could come because I wasn't the sort of monster who'd keep his daughter from her mother, but she'd signed over custody and left the country, all for a man. I would not be simply returning things to how they had been before.

"Can I, Daddy?" Evanne looked at me with those big blue eyes of hers. "Can I invite the whole class?"

"We'll talk about it more after we get home," I promised. "How about on the flight, you start thinking of ideas?"

"Great!" Keli said brightly. "We girls will make up a list of everything we can have."

I caught a flicker of confusion in Evanne's eyes before she let Keli pull her into a hug. I hated this. What little girl wouldn't want to think that the last couple months had just been a vacation and her mom hadn't left her? And while I didn't like the idea of deceiving her, I couldn't bring myself to deliver the harsh reality that Keli had chosen a man over her daughter.

I'd deal with whatever Keli had been trying to do this week, pretending as if nothing had changed. No, I amended. She wasn't behaving as if nothing had changed because, before she left, this wasn't how things had been between us. She was behaving as if she, Evanne, and I were all...family.

What the bloody hell was going on in that woman's head?

THIRTEEN

LUMEN

The week had gone faster than I'd anticipated, probably because I'd kept myself busy. Now, it was Sunday afternoon, and I felt like I'd accomplished a lot. I'd done some tutoring at the group home, thoroughly cleaned every inch of the apartment, answered phones at Real Life Bodywork for a few hours on Thursday, and gotten so far ahead in my lesson plans that I'd probably regret it if I had to redo more than a couple hours a week.

The sense of accomplishment I felt, however, did nothing to alleviate the way my stomach had grown steadily more twisted as time passed without me hearing from Alec. I told myself he was busy, and my head knew that was the most likely explanation for his silence, but the part of me that had never completely healed from my

101

parents' abandonment could be obnoxiously loud at times.

I wouldn't have to wait much longer for answers. I'd be back in the classroom tomorrow, and Evanne would most likely want to tell me about all of the things she and Alec had done while visiting her grandparents. I'd liked Evanne's grandmother, Theresa, when I first met her. In a way, she'd reminded me of Lihua, and I imagined that, in their own way, Alec's family was like the Jins. Full of their own quirks and squabbles, but at the core, a fiercely loyal and loving group.

The big question was what I would do if Evanne didn't offer up anything about her trip that would tell me why Alec hadn't called or texted for several days. I already hated that I was obsessing over this, and to make it worse, the thought kept popping in my head that it wouldn't be too difficult or out of line to ask Evanne how Alec was doing, especially if I did it when I asked the entire class how they were feeling about the prior week. Unless we were instructed not to talk to our students about the shooting, that was one of the first things I already had on my schedule for tomorrow.

Just as I was beating myself up over how completely unprofessional that would be, someone knocked on my door. I went to it, wondering who it could be since Mai was working, and she tried to schedule times when Hob was already working so the two of them had an easier time seeing each other. No one else really visited. Unless it was the super, of course. He came around each spring and fall to ask if there were any repairs that needed to be made before the weather changed.

I wracked my brains for anything we needed to have done, but every thought I had flew out of my mind the moment I opened the door and found Alec standing there, looking rumpled and sexy.

"Hello, lass."

I took a step back and motioned for him to come inside, still too surprised to speak. He'd said he'd let me know when he and Evanne arrived home, and I'd taken that as a courtesy so I wouldn't worry about them while they were traveling. Nothing would've made me even consider him coming over to tell me in person.

"You're back." I could've kicked myself for how completely moronic that statement sounded. "How was your flight?"

He closed the door and then came to me, ignoring the question. My mouth went dry at the sight of his eyes blazing, and then his lips were on mine, and that was all that mattered. His hands were hot on my cheeks, and my body thrummed in anticipation of that touch elsewhere.

When we finally broke to breathe, his hands dropped to my hips, and I curled my fingers in his shirt, neither of us apparently ready to let go. All of the doubts I'd had were melted away faster and more cleanly than they would have been had I pushed for a conversation.

"Is Mai here?" he asked, his voice rough.

"She's at work."

His fingers flexed on my hips. "Evanne is with her mother for the afternoon."

A jolt of surprise accompanied his words, but I managed to keep it from my face. I didn't know much about Evanne's mother, but it wasn't my place to ask. Not with things between Alec and me still so new. I allowed myself to simply be happy that he'd come to me when he had a few free hours rather than going to work or just relaxing by himself, both of which would've been completely understandable after him having been gone all week.

"I missed you." I risked the whisper.

Alec's response was to take my mouth again, the last of what he'd been holding back breaking through. He hadn't said the words, but in every line of his body, I could feel how much he'd missed me too. That was more than good enough for me.

His hands moved to my hair, yanking out my pony-tail, and taking a few strands with it. The little bites of pain in my scalp just fed my arousal, and I stretched up on my toes to try to limit the distance between us. His tongue swept between my lips, and my knees went weak. Damn, but the man could kiss.

I leaned into him, hooking my fingers in the waistband of his pants. His skin was hot against the backs of my fingers, and I wanted more. More skin, more flesh, more of him against me and inside me. I slid my hands around his back, splaying my fingers over the bunching muscles there. When his teeth scraped across my bottom lip, I scratched his back, and he made that primal, low, growling sound that instantly made me wet.

"*Mo nighean bhan*," he groaned against my mouth. "I need you."

"Then take me."

The words were barely out of my mouth before we were both on the floor. He rolled me onto my stomach and pulled me up on my hands and knees, all with a speed that left my head spinning. I didn't need long to get my footing, metaphorically speaking, because Alec's hands were sliding over my hips and taking my pants with them.

A brush of cool air caressed my overheated skin as he slid my panties over my ass and down to my knees. He palmed one cheek, then brought his hand down on it with a sharp crack. I gasped, a warm tingle spreading out across my skin from where his hand had made contact.

"I dinnae ken if I can be...gentle."

I looked over my shoulder, the sheer intensity of his expression sending a shudder through me. "Don't be. Show me how much you missed me."

The condom was already in his hand, and he wasted no time putting it on. Then he was pushing inside me, thick and long, and I was cursing, my body shaking. I was wet, but there hadn't been enough foreplay for this to be easy. I didn't mind. In fact, as his body curled over mine, the throbbing between my legs made me feel more complete than I had all week.

"Touch yourself, lass." Alec nipped my shoulder through my shirt.

I reached underneath me, and as he withdrew, my fingers slid over my clit. He drove forward hard enough to make me cry out, and then his fingers tangled in my hair, pulling my head up. I stroked that sensitive bundle of nerves as Alec pounded into me. Electric shocks and pleasure combined with all the loneliness and emptiness I'd felt over the last few days, winding me up.

"Fuck, Lumen, you feel so good."

"Faster." I rocked back, and his next thrust went impossibly deep. White spots danced in front of my eyes, and I felt myself teetering on the edge. My fingers moved faster, the friction making my eyes roll back.

"Come for me, lass. I need to feel you come."

My muscles clenched, body stiffened, and I trembled there in that space just before release...then came with a muffled scream. My arm buckled, and I barely caught myself before I face-planted. Alec drove into me faster now, my name coming in grunts and groans until he slammed into me and held there, his cock pulsing inside me as he came.

He slumped onto my back, and we both collapsed onto the carpet. I was going to have some uncomfortable marks, but it was well worth it, and not only for physical reasons.

He'd missed me.

He stirred behind me, easing himself out of me with a hiss. He kissed the side of my throat. "Now that I've taken the edge off, I'll pay you the proper attention you deserve."

It appeared we weren't done yet.

FOURTEEN
LUMEN

GOING BACK TO SCHOOL WAS EASIER THAN I'D thought it would be, and I knew part of that was because I no longer had all those worries and questions about Alec clouding my mind. He hadn't explained, exactly, why he hadn't gotten back to me, but we hadn't exactly spent much time talking either. In fact, in the three hours we'd spent together yesterday afternoon, we'd had enough sex to leave my entire body sore today.

I smiled as I made my way back to my classroom after our short teachers' meeting. It hadn't taken long for us to confirm that we were okay and Principal McKenna to tell us that we should determine what and how much our students needed to know. After that, it was business as usual.

I was still straightening out my rows when I heard

someone at the door. My smile faded as I saw a familiar but unwelcome face.

"Vice Principal Harvey."

"Lumen." He smiled that smarmy smile that made my skin crawl. "I tried to catch you after the meeting, but you scampered out of there before I could talk to you."

Yes, because I didn't want to talk to you.

The words echoed in my head, but I didn't say them. I might not have had much in the way of self-control when it came to Alec McCrae, but I definitely knew how and when to keep my mouth shut.

"I just wanted to ask how you're doing."

If I hadn't interacted with the vice principal before, I might've thought that was genuine concern, but I knew how to look for the lechery beneath the mask. Still, I kept my voice professional. "I'm fine, thank you."

"Are you sure? I mean, I can stay here with you all day, make sure you're safe." He came a few feet into the classroom.

I moved behind my desk on the pretense of checking my lesson plan book and hoped he didn't realize I was trying to keep something between us. "I appreciate the offer, but it's not necessary." When he looked like he was going to argue, I added, "I think it might actually scare the children, having the vice principal in here during class time."

He nodded, trying to pretend he wasn't annoyed. "Oh, you missed Principal McKenna saying that there's going to be a meeting this coming Saturday evening to address new security measures that've been put in place. Parents and the community are invited to come, but all faculty are expected to be there."

"Okay. Thank you." I turned my attention back to my desk and hoped he'd take the hint and leave.

When he cleared his throat, I sighed but was saved from having to hear him try to find reasons to stay in my room when two of my students appeared in the doorway, one with their father and the other with their nanny. Grateful for the excuse to ignore him, I immediately went to talk to them. After I was done with them, Skylar and his mother arrived, and Harvey finally figured out that he wouldn't be alone with me any time soon. He left, leaving me free to focus all my attention on the people who mattered.

During the time I'd been with Skylar's mom, a few kids had come in on their own. I went around to them and made it back to the door in time for Evanne to rush in and throw her arms around me.

"I missed you, Ms. Browne," she declared.

"I missed you too," I said, smoothing my hand over her hair.

Unable to help it, I glanced up at the doorway, half expecting Alec to appear, but he didn't. I told myself not to be disappointed, and it mostly worked. I reminded myself that he'd taken nearly an entire week off work, and while he could work remotely on some things, he had to have been anxious about all of the things he hadn't been able to handle while he'd been away. Besides, we'd spent time together yesterday.

"Did you have fun with your grandparents?" I asked as Evanne released me.

"I did. And then Mommy came, and that made it even better."

Mommy?

Alec had said yesterday that Evanne had been with her mother, but he hadn't mentioned that Keli had been with them all week. Based on what he'd told me, Keli had been overseas with a new boyfriend. It made sense that she was back. After all, her daughter had been through something possibly traumatic.

Any decent mother would've wanted to make sure their child was okay, and despite what she'd done by leaving Evanne with Alec, Keli was, at the very least, a decent mother. I just hadn't realized that she'd been with them while they'd visited his parents. I'd assumed – foolishly, perhaps – that she'd been here waiting for them when they'd gotten back.

"She wanted to surprise me," Evanne continued, "and it worked because I didn't know she was coming to Grand-da and Grandma's house at all. Even Daddy was surprised."

Unless Alec had been playing along, that at least answered my question about whether or not he'd invited Keli to join them. It didn't, however, ease the way my stomach was churning. I didn't think Alec had cheated on me with Keli, but it bothered me that he hadn't mentioned her. I didn't want him to ever feel like he had to hide things from me, or that I'd be the kind of woman who wanted him to keep Evanne from her mother simply because Keli was his ex.

"Grandma and Aunt Paris and me all went shopping." Evanne motioned to her outfit. "We had lots of fun getting me new clothes, and then we baked a lot. Mommy helped us make tacos. One day was really hot so we went swimming in Grand-da's pool. Well, not *really* hot, but enough that Daddy said I could swim."

"It sounds like you had fun." I smiled. "We're going to draw pictures in art class of what we did last week, and I bet you'll have a lot of great things to draw."

"I will," she said, clapping her hands together. "I got

to go see Mommy's hotel yesterday, and she has a pool too. Does that count as what I did last week?"

"Of course." I gave her shoulder a light squeeze. "Why don't you put your things where they belong and then go have a seat, all right? I need to talk to these parents before class starts." I motioned toward the couple patiently waiting with their daughter.

"Okay." Evanne practically bounced to the coat hooks.

"Good morning," I said as I turned toward another set of parents and fixed a polite smile on my face. "Are there any questions or concerns I can address for you?"

Even as I reassured students and parents alike, I couldn't help worrying about what was going on with Evanne. From what I understood, Keli had never been neglectful or abusive, and while I might not be able to understand a parent choosing to do something that would result in them giving up complete custody of their child to the other parent, it wasn't as if she'd dropped Evanne off at a group home or DCFS. Things could've been handled better, but Keli wasn't really a *bad* mother.

I couldn't, however, bring myself to think of her as a *good* mother, either. If she'd wanted to alter the custody arrangement, I wouldn't have had such an issue with it, but she hadn't simply shifted things so that she had a more joint-custody agreement. She'd left the country.

Evanne had gone from living primarily with her mother and having visitation with her father a few days a month to suddenly living with her dad and not seeing her mom at all.

Maybe I couldn't see things as clearly as I needed to, my past clouding my judgment when it came to what a parent should or shouldn't do. No kid who spent time in foster care had zero baggage. The size and type varied from person to person, but it was there all the same. Parental abandonment was mine, and I hadn't needed a child psychology course to tell me that.

But this wasn't my business. I needed to ask myself what I would have done if another student had been in this situation. A student whose father I *wasn't* sleeping with. I couldn't show Evanne special treatment, no matter what Alec and I were to each other. In the classroom, she was one of my students, the same as Skylar or Mercedes or Julian.

Outside the classroom, I didn't know what this meant for Alec and me, whether Keli's return to Seattle was something that would affect our relationship or not. That was something I'd have to discuss with Alec, but I couldn't split my focus. I had to set this aside and focus on teaching. Everything else would come later.

FIFTEEN

ALEC

I'D NEVER ANTICIPATED THE END OF THE WEEK AS much as I had these past few days. Work hadn't suffered as much as I'd feared it would, and if I had allowed others to take over more, I would have had even less to do. Delegating more wasn't something I would have ever considered before, but having Evanne living with me had changed things already. Lumen becoming a part of my life had begun to alter my world view even more so.

The moment Evanne had begged me to let her spend a few hours with Keli the Sunday afternoon after we returned from San Ramon, I'd immediately known what I wanted to do with those newly freed hours. After the week I'd had, I was glad I'd taken the opportunity. Between work and Keli's unexpected presence, I'd barely had time for a few short phone calls to Lumen, and none of them had done a thing to give me even the slightest relief.

Also nagging at the back of my mind all week was the fact that Keli and I needed to have a discussion regarding her sudden return to Evanne's life, but I hadn't been able to get her alone. I needed to know why Keli had returned, how long she planned to stay, and what it meant for our new arrangement with Evanne. None of those things, however, needed to be discussed in front of our daughter. Not until we had answers for her.

Perhaps I should have set the expectation that Evanne would be spending no exclusive time with Keli until we resolved the issues. Had I told Keli that, however, I ran the risk of her putting Evanne in the middle of everything, intentionally or not. That meant when, halfway through the week, Keli had asked Evanne if she'd wanted to spend the night at the hotel where Keli had been staying, I had agreed, so long as Evanne was back by Sunday morning.

While having a free weekend wasn't my intention or desire, it was something I had and intended to use. When I'd mentioned it to Lumen, I'd hoped to invite her over to spend the weekend with me. She had suggested something different, or at least something different to precede time alone.

A date.

And not just any date. I was about to go on a double date with Lumen, Mai, and Mai's boyfriend, Hob. I could probably count on one hand the number of double dates I'd been on in my entire life, and none of them in the last ten years. All of them had also been attempts by my siblings to get me to be more social.

At least I had met both Mai and Hob before. Not in any official capacity, but it was something. Contrary to what most people thought, I wasn't calm and confident in every situation. I simply chose to put myself only in those situations where I had the knowledge to carry myself in the manner I wished to be seen.

This was not one of those situations. Mai had insisted on planning everything, which meant I had no idea how to dress or prepare. This was the excuse, at least, that I used to explain why it had taken me nearly twice the time to get ready as it usually did. Dress slacks, a short-sleeved dress shirt, and a suit jacket shouldn't have taken me this long to choose.

When Lumen's eyes lit up the moment she opened the door, it was worth all the frustration. The sexy little black dress she was wearing helped too.

"You look amazing!"

After I stepped inside the apartment, she went up on her tiptoes and kissed my cheek. "Not too shabby yourself, lass." I put my hands on her hips and pulled her against me for a better greeting.

Her mouth was as sweet as ever, lips soft as they parted. The tip of my tongue traced her bottom lip before delving inside. I lost myself in the taste and feel of her, drowning in the sea of her until a not-so-discreet cough reminded us that we weren't alone.

Still, I kept one hand on her waist as I turned toward the sound. Mai grinned at us, clearly enjoying the sight of her roommate blushing. Lumen didn't pull away, though. If anything, she leaned against me more, and then she put her hand on my stomach, making it necessary for me to think of other things to prevent getting an erection right there.

Mud.

Haggis.

That infernal song from the winter movie Evanne insisted on watching every day she'd spent with me over her Christmas break last year.

That last one effectively killed my arousal.

"Hob's meeting us there," Mai said, looking decidedly disappointed. "He had to finish up some paperwork before he could leave."

"I have a driver waiting downstairs," I said. "I thought it might be nice for none of us to have to worry about whether or not we wish to indulge in something to drink."

"Considerate." Mai held out her arms. "Now, how do I look?"

"Lovely," I answered honestly. As a man, I could appreciate her beauty, but it also stirred nothing inside me.

How different my life would be now if she had been the one I met that night. She probably would have given me a black eye for my 'happy ending' request, and she definitely would have made sure I paid before she kicked me out. I wouldn't have gone back. And despite how pretty she was, I wouldn't have been enamored with her.

"Good answer," Mai said. She smiled as she came over and took my free arm. "Now, let's see what sort of car you brought me."

I didn't say much as the three of us made our way out to my car, but the walk was not a silent one. Mai kept up an easy flow of chatter as we went and continued it in the car. With Lumen tucked under my arm, I was happy to simply listen to the two of them, though she definitely said less than her roommate. I felt like I was getting to see a third side to Lumen. She wasn't someone who pretended to be something else, but she did present different parts of her personality depending on her role.

As a teacher, she softened her humor and her passion, tempered it to fit the education of third graders. With me, I saw a sexual side that still seemed to surprise her, a woman realizing the power she held. Now, I saw a more relaxed side of her, the comfort that came with knowing the other person had seen you at your best and worst. Mai was Lumen's family, and Lumen became herself in the same way I did when I was with my family.

Perhaps even more, I admitted. At some point in my past, I might have been free of pretense around my family, but recently, that had not been the case. My need for them to see me as strong, in control, and independent, wasn't an easy façade to maintain.

In a cruel twist of irony, just as I was thinking about façades, we pulled up to a restaurant I'd never been to before. I should have been paying more attention to the name Mai had given the driver, but I'd been too preoccupied with how much I'd missed the feel of Lumen's body next to mine.

She appeared to be just as aware of me as I was of her, and I felt more than saw her concern when I tensed. Instead of addressing it, however, I exited the car without waiting for the driver to open the door for me. He went to the other side for Mai, and I held out a hand to Lumen.

"Have you been here before?" I asked as we walked around to where Mai was waiting.

Lumen shook her head. "Hob recommended it. Did you have somewhere else in mind?"

"Just curious." It was a half-truth at best, but it would have to do as I wasn't inclined to share the rest of what was behind my question.

Mai's boyfriend was waiting for us inside. My initial impression of him when I'd first seen him had been *hipster,* and even in clothes similar to mine, that label still seemed applicable. Lumen had mentioned that he was a resident with goals of becoming a first-rate pediatrician, which meant we most likely shared a strong work ethic, but most likely little else.

"Armani Hobson," he said, holding out a hand. "But everyone calls me Hob."

"Alec McCrae."

He had a firm handshake but wasn't trying to squeeze my hand in some macho show of force. His eyes were cat-green and shrewd, as if he was studying me prior to deciding what he thought of me. The protective way he greeted Lumen told me what I needed to know. He wasn't trying to show me up, but rather to watch out for Lumen in the same way my brothers and I watched out for our sisters.

As we were led to our seats, I kept my hand on the

small of Lumen's back, the touch centering me, grounding me. I'd never been the sort of person who needed much physical contact, but with her, it was different. If she was near me, I wanted to touch her.

"Do you drink wine, Alec?" Hob asked as he pulled out Mai's chair for her.

I did the same for Lumen as I answered, "I do."

"Would you like to see the wine selection?" the hostess asked with a polite smile.

I shook my head and hoped the expression on my face didn't look as wooden as it felt. "Whatever you'd like. I'll buy the first one."

Hob didn't even glance at the menu as he ordered a Santa Julia Malbec. A red wine, then. I filed away the name. As the others picked up their menus, I did the same. Small talk buzzed around me as the others shared about their days. My throat was dry, and I gulped down half of my water, hoping the waiter would be back quickly to take our orders.

As if my thoughts had conjured him, the waiter appeared. "Is everyone ready, or do you need more time?"

Hob nodded. "I'm good."

"Me too," Mai said.

Lumen lifted an eyebrow at me. "Alec?"

"Yes, I'm ready." When the waiter looked at me, I

cut my gaze across the table to Hob, expecting him to take the lead.

He did without question. "I'll take the flatbread of the week and the French onion mac and cheese."

The waiter turned to Mai next. "I'll take the venison meatloaf."

Neither of those things appealed to me.

"I'll have the fried Cornish game hen," Lumen said.

After taking down her sides, the waiter looked at me. "I'll have the same as her."

"Excellent choices," the waiter said.

I held out my menu along with the others and tried not to be annoyed at the fact that I wasn't really in the mood for game hen tonight. I would've preferred a steak or maybe pasta. If we did this again, I'd offer to choose the restaurant, and we'd go to one of my favorite places. I'd even offer to cover the bill.

But that was another time and place. This was here and now, which meant I couldn't spend time brooding over the food. I cared about Lumen, and these two were her family. If I wanted her in my life, I needed to get to know them.

"Lumen hasn't told me," I said, reaching for my wine glass. "How did the two of you meet?"

SIXTEEN
LUMEN

SOMETHING HAD BEEN OFF WITH ALEC SINCE WE'D gotten to the restaurant. He wasn't being rude or anything, but he seemed annoyed for some reason. Not so much that Mai or Hob noticed, but either he was getting worse at hiding what he felt, or I was getting better at reading him. Maybe a little of both.

The food and service were excellent. I only had a single glass of wine, but that had more to do with my lack of fondness for wine than it did about the quality. At least, I assumed it did. The others didn't complain about it, anyway.

Mai was brilliant, and once I admitted that to her, I was going to owe her big time. She asked questions, told stories, basically filled the silence when it threatened to become awkward. Instead of focusing on things she wanted to know about Alec, she talked about her own life, posed questions to Hob and me, tried to keep the conversation all inclusive. It seemed to be working too.

"I told them to be careful, but no one listens to the resident," Hob continued his story. "So they pick this kid up and, just like I warned, he vomits all over them."

"Really, Hob? *That's* the story you decide to tell at dinner?" Mai smacked his arm. "You couldn't talk about the boy who got the pencil eraser stuck in his nose?"

"His vomit had glitter in it!" Hob said with a laugh. "Come on, that's hilarious!"

"You and I have very different ideas of what's funny," I said, shaking my head.

"Like your stories are any better," Hob countered. "I still cringe when you two bring up that guy who refused to use a towel."

"Not as much as we cringed," Mai said. "Trust me, that was not a pretty sight to be walking in on."

"Thanks for sharing that experience with me," I said dryly. "It was once in a lifetime."

"What about you, Alec?" Mai asked. "Or is the business world not as entertaining?"

He gave Mai a half-smile. "I'm afraid I don't have many fun days at work. Mostly spreadsheets and talking to the board."

"I'll bet your daughter's a trip, right?" Mai said. "Lumen says she's a precocious one."

And just like that, he really smiled, one of those big smiles that made my insides go all warm and gooey. I loved seeing that expression on his face. That was a special one, just for Evanne. No matter how closed-off he could be with his emotions, he never closed himself off from her. He was a good man, but a great father, even if he didn't always think so.

"She is a canty one," he said, his accent thickening. "Full of laughter and a wee bit of mischief."

"Lumen, will you loan him to me," Mai said suddenly. "I just want him to read things in that accent. I promise I'll give him back."

We laughed, Alec included, but something in his eyes made me doubt that his heart was really in that humor. I needed to get him back to talking about Evanne. Maybe then he'd be comfortable again.

Or more comfortable, anyway.

By the time we left the restaurant, he seemed at ease, relaxed either by the passage of time or the couple glasses of wine he'd had. Judging by the much-stronger alcohol I'd seen him consume before, I was betting on the former. That was good. I didn't want him to feel ill at ease with my friends. At least Hob hadn't drunk too much to drive himself and Mai back to the apartment, so Alec and I were alone for the ride home.

"Do you still want to come back to my place?" he asked as we settled in the back of the car.

"If you want me there." I probably could have told him that, yes, I wanted to go home with him. I wanted to spend the night, have him make love to me. But I didn't want to be the one making that call considering how unsettled I'd felt most of the night. Maybe it was cowardly of me, but I needed to be sure he wanted me there. I didn't want to force myself in where I wasn't wanted.

He leaned closer and pressed his lips against my ear. "I always want you, lass."

The hand on my knee slid higher up my leg, taking my dress with it. His fingers sent a wave of fire licking up my skin, and I caught my breath. Teeth fastened onto my earlobe, and I grabbed the front of his jacket. My eyes closed, attention focused on the heat of his breath against my skin, the soft pads of his fingers creeping up the inside of my thigh.

"I cannae wait to get you properly alone." He kissed the side of my neck. "Slide my tongue deep inside you, taste you until you scream."

"Sounds good to me," I said breathlessly.

He laughed, and the sound vibrated on my skin,

sending a shiver through me. "You ken what would sound good to me? You begging me to let you come."

"That doesn't sound like something I would do," I teased.

He chuckled, low and deep. "Perhaps I will have to prove you wrong."

"And just how – ahhh..." My sentence became lost when the tip of his index finger traced up my slit and pressed over my clit.

"I think I can suss something out."

NOTE TO SELF: *never* tell Alec McCrae that he was wrong. He took it as a challenge.

My declaration that I wouldn't beg to come was the reason I was currently sprawled on his bed, completely naked, with him stretched out between my legs. He'd used his mouth and fingers to bring me to the brink of orgasm three times already but stopped each time before I'd reached it. Now, my entire body was a mass of frustration, my nerves screaming that they were on fire. I was desperate for release...but not *quite* desperate enough to beg.

"How are you doing, lass?"

I glared at him. "You'll have to do better than that."

He raised his eyebrow, the movement making the scar through it stand out more than usual. "I suppose I'll have to be trying something new."

That low, primal part of me throbbed in anticipation. I'd been a virgin before him, which meant anything he hadn't done with me yet would be new, but I had a feeling he had something particular in mind.

The tip of his tongue flicked against my swollen clit, and I caught my breath. For someone who was fairly quiet, he sure knew how to use his mouth. Two fingers slid inside me, and he matched it stroke for stroke with his tongue. I fisted the sheets, hips trying to move but held in place with the hand on my stomach.

He curled his fingers, and I cried out as they pressed against my g-spot. The intensity of sensations coursing through me nearly brought me to tears, and I knew if I didn't come this time, I would beg.

And I didn't care.

His tongue circled my clit, and the fingers inside me relentlessly pushed me toward the pinnacle, but just before I could reach it, he moved back, cutting off all contact.

"No!" I slammed my hands on the mattress. "Not again!"

He traced my opening with one finger and lightly blew on my clit. I shivered. "Aye, lass. Again. Unless..."

I knew what he wanted, and I cursed him for it. "Just wait," I promised. "When it's my turn, I'm going to make you sorry."

He grinned at me, and it was that smile rather than my own need that finally broke me.

"Please, Alec. Please let me come." I reached down and ran my fingers through his hair. "Please. I need you."

"Good lass."

He wrapped his lips around my clit and sucked on that bundle of nerves hard enough to make my eyes roll back. I was prepared for him to finish me off that way, but then I felt a slick finger some place new. A single digit circled my anus, the prickles of panic it caused overwhelmed by the intensity of what his mouth was doing. I felt him hesitate, and I nodded once. Maybe I was riding a high, but everything he'd done to me so far had felt good. I trusted him.

He pushed his finger into my ass, not all the way, but enough to send me soaring. I cried out his name, my back arching as his finger and mouth made me forget anything else existed. I was on fire, every cell burning with the sort of fury that threatened to consume, to turn to ash everything in its path.

I was dimly aware that he'd moved, and the shudders wracking my body now were the aftereffects of one of the biggest orgasms I'd ever had. I heard a ripping sound, and I forced my eyes open as the bed shifted underneath me. My eyes met his, and then he was inside me.

"Alec!" I grabbed his shoulders as I came again. Or still. I wasn't entirely sure which, and it really didn't matter.

"Lumen, *mhurninn*."

He covered my mouth with his, tongue plundering even as he rode my body. Every thrust sent another wave of pleasure washing over and through me until it was too much. I couldn't breathe or speak or do anything but cling to him until he finally stiffened above me, his cock swelling impossibly inside me moments before he came. He held himself there, muscles tense, and I wrapped my legs around him, using my weak limbs to coax him down until his full, comfortable weight rested on me.

My whole life, I'd wondered where I fit, where I belonged, and here, in this moment, I couldn't help thinking that maybe I'd finally found my place.

SEVENTEEN

ALEC

THERE WAS SOMETHING TO BE SAID FOR WAKING UP with a warm body that smelled like vanilla. I hadn't slept this well since...well, since the last time Lumen and I had slept in the same bed.

Even though it was Saturday morning, my body woke me not long after six, telling me that I should have already been up and about. I'd essentially worked every Saturday from the time I was sixteen up until the time Evanne had been born, and then it had become every other Saturday until she'd moved in. But it wasn't as if having Evanne here meant I was able to sleep much later than I did when I was working.

Today, however, I had no pressing need to get up. Well, aside from a need to use the bathroom.

I managed to get out of the bed without waking

Lumen, and after I came out of the bathroom, I went back to my bedroom. She was still asleep, and for a moment, I stood in the doorway between the two rooms.

Lumen was twenty-four, but asleep, she looked younger. Honey blonde hair spilled over my pillow, and her porcelain skin practically glowed in the dim light. She'd pulled the sheets and blanket up around her, covering the body I knew as well as my own. Neither of us had bothered dressing after we'd cleaned up, and as I climbed back under the covers, her soft skin warmed mine. I wrapped an arm around her, and she rolled over, her breasts pressed to my side. Her bare thigh brushed against my cock, and blood rushed south.

In a bit, I'd get up and make her breakfast, I decided. While I might have liked to wake her in a more sensual way, we'd had sex more than once last night, and I knew she might be too sensitive for that to be a good idea. Before I started to cook, however, I wanted to take some time to enjoy this moment.

The next thing I knew, the sound of a door opening jarred me from sleep. The clock on the bedside table said it was a little after eight-thirty, but that just told me I'd most likely dozed off. It didn't, however, explain why I heard voices coming from my living room.

I was out of bed and halfway to the door when I realized two things at once. First, I was naked. Second, the voices I heard were Keli and Evanne.

What the hell?

I grabbed a pair of pants and a shirt, pulling on the latter as I left the bedroom. I closed the door behind me and hoped I could figure out what was happening before Lumen woke up. Evanne wouldn't freak out if she saw Lumen, but neither Lumen nor I had planned on this.

And who knew what Keli would do.

"Daddy!" Evanne threw her arms around me. "I had so much fun last night with Mommy that she said we could come home for breakfast and tell you all about it."

I returned my daughter's hug but looked at Keli over Evanne's head. "How did you get in here?" I kept my voice calm, but inside, I was seething.

Keli held up a key. "You gave me a key and the code, remember?"

I narrowed my eyes. "For emergencies."

"And what do you think this is, silly?" Keli giggled.

My eyes went wide. Where had *that* come from?

"How, *exactly*, is this an emergency?" I spoke through gritted teeth.

"Because our daughter wanted to tell you about how our sleepover went." Keli moved closer and put her hand on Evanne's head. "Right, sweetie?"

"We went swimming," Evanne announced. "And there were kids there from *Utah*."

"I'll go put your things in your room," Keli said. "You can put them away after we have breakfast."

I opened my mouth to ask who the *we* in her statement was...and then remembered I had a naked woman in my bed. "Keli!"

She stopped two steps away from the hallway and turned, a confused expression on her face.

"Evanne needs to take care of her own things." It was the maddest thing I could have said, but it was also the first thing that popped into my head.

"I think we can make an exception, Alec. Why don't you and Evanne go start breakfast, and I'll be right there."

"Can we make pancakes?" Evanne tugged on my arm. "And I can tell you all about George and Keenan."

Before I could respond to either of them, Lumen appeared behind Keli and my heart about stopped. The world went still, and I saw it all in minute detail. Bag over her shoulder, Lumen was dressed in casual clothes and her hair was pulled back in a ponytail, she looked like any other woman on her way to the gym on a Saturday morning. But coming down the stairs, there was absolutely no way that Keli didn't know why Lumen was here, even if she didn't know who Lumen was.

"Ms. Browne!" Evanne ran to Lumen, who smiled even as her cheeks flooded with color.

"Good morning." She hugged Evanne. "It's good to see you."

"You can have breakfast with us!" Evanne practically sang as she jumped up and down, clapping her hands in total glee. "We're going to make pancakes!"

"No, honey, I can't. I have someplace I need to be." Lumen didn't even look at me or at Keli, for that matter. "I'll see you Monday, okay?"

"All right." Evanne nodded. She straightened her shoulders like she did when she tried to be overly formal. "Let me walk you to the door." Then she grinned, and I saw all the humor she'd gotten from her Uncle Brody.

As the two of them walked toward the front door, Keli looked at me. "Ms. Browne? As in our daughter's _teacher_, Ms. Browne?"

I held up a hand. "Not now."

Instead of arguing with me as I expected, she broke out in a smile. "Of course not. We have to talk, but Evanne's going to be back in a minute, and we have to prioritize."

She was right. There were more important things for me to be discussing with her, not the least of which was the question she had managed to avoid answering for nearly two weeks.

"Why are you back?"

Keli looked hurt, but I saw a familiar glint in her eyes that told me she wasn't going to be completely forthcoming. "The whole time I was gone, I missed my family. Alessandro couldn't understand that just sitting around all day in a place where I didn't know anyone wasn't what I wanted anymore."

That had the ring of at least some small truth.

"We need to make things work, Alec. For Evanne's sake."

Just as I thought I couldn't be shocked anymore, Keli managed to do it again when she leaned in and kissed me.

Fuck my life.

EIGHTEEN
LUMEN

MAI WAS WORKING, WHICH MEANT I CAME HOME TO an empty apartment. Considering the chaos that my thoughts and emotions had become, solitude was a good thing. Granted, it meant that I didn't have anyone to help distract me, but that also meant I didn't have Mai trying to pick my brain, something at which she excelled.

Voices had woken me this morning, and for a few seconds, I'd thought Alec had turned on the television. Then two of the voices registered, and I realized the third had to be Evanne's mom. I'd thought Alec had said Evanne would be with Keli until later tonight, but perhaps I'd misunderstood.

My face flushed as I thought about how foolish I must've looked when Alec had woken up to find me still next to him – and naked, of course. Spending the night had been a poor decision on my part. Sure, Evanne had seen us together once before, but I didn't want to make a habit of it, not until Alec and I were on more solid footing. One date where he'd met Mai and Hob hardly meant we were getting to know each other's families. And I had no idea what Keli knew about me either.

Unless that was the reason Alec hadn't woken me up when he'd realized I was still there. He'd hoped I'd sleep through Evanne being dropped off and not have to explain to Keli why another woman was in his home. I'd only been able to think of two reasons why a man wouldn't want his ex to know he'd had someone sleeping over. One, he'd known her reaction wouldn't be a good one, or two, he hadn't wanted her to think he'd moved on because he hadn't.

The first I could accept, but the second had been what had spurred me into action. I'd grabbed my bag and had taken the first clothes I'd laid my hands on. I hadn't done anything wrong, and Evanne had seen Alec and me together before, but that had done little to calm me.

The adults had gone silent the moment I'd stepped into the living room, but Evanne had come to me immediately. I'd been too much of a coward to look at Alec's face, but me making an excuse not to stay when Evanne had asked had been more about not wanting to prolong an awkward situation to the point where Evanne would have noticed that something was wrong. And as much as I hated admitting it, something *was* wrong.

Keli was back, and she was Evanne's mother. I didn't know what her return meant for Alec and my relationship. I didn't know what it meant for Alec's custody of Evanne, or how all of this would affect my student. Then there was the guilt I felt for being worried about Alec and me at all when the person we should have all been concerned with was Evanne. She'd made absolutely no decisions that had led to this point, but she'd have to live with the consequences as much as any of us. Probably more.

I needed to get my shit together.

Evanne deserved a teacher who was wholly focused on her well-being. All of my students deserved that, and there was a meeting in a few hours that would play a role in the safety of everyone at Kurt Wright. I couldn't go into it still consumed with trying to figure out what'd happened or how to react, especially since I couldn't really do the latter without the former. That meant I needed to put on my big girl panties and be a grown-up about things.

The first step to that was taking a shower to get rid of

Alec's scent all over me. Maybe then I could think more clearly.

When I walked into the school that evening, I felt much more like the professional educator I was and less like the inexperienced neophyte...which I *also* was. Needless to say, Mai had gotten home in time to help me with my clothes. I wore the outfit I'd gotten for my interview: black slacks and matching suit jacket with a nice white dress shirt. Hair in a ponytail and minimal makeup went with my sensible heels to complete the ensemble. Mai had lamented the lack of fun but didn't argue, so I considered it a win.

The first people I saw in the assembly hall – Kurt Wright would never use something as crass as a gymnasium for a meeting of this magnitude – were Mr. and Mrs. Crenshaw, but since their son Skylar wasn't with them, I didn't feel much guilt for ducking behind my colleague, Mr. Buchannan. Every conversation I'd had with Mrs. Crenshaw had been a list of all the things I was doing wrong in regard to her son's education. Mr. Crenshaw had barely said a word to me, and I was under the impression that he didn't talk much.

"Avoiding the Crenshaws?" Mr. Buchannan asked as he turned toward me.

The grin on his face told me that he wasn't admonishing me for it. He was the sort of man who fit the physical stereotype of a gym teacher, but after talking to him for ten minutes at the beginning of the school year, I'd felt guilty for making assumptions based on his looks. Massive and almost scary, he was a former Marine now in his mid-fifties, and he just celebrated his fifth anniversary with a man he'd met in the service. He was also one of the most intelligent and articulate men I'd ever met.

"What gave me away?" I asked.

"Probably the fact that I'd be doing the same thing if they weren't on the warpath for Principal McKenna." He rubbed his bald head. "Rumor is they're furious that no one will tell them the name of the kid who had the gun."

"It never should have happened," I said, "but at least this was an accident and not malicious. We have the opportunity to address an issue without having to suffer the consequences other schools have had to face."

Just then, out of the corner of my eye, I saw Alec enter, and my heart gave an unsteady thump that immediately became a sinking sensation when Keli appeared at his side, Evanne holding both of their hands. I shouldn't have been surprised that Keli was here. Evanne was her daughter, and from what I understood, it'd been Keli's decision to enroll Evanne at Kurt Wright.

I also shouldn't have been jealous that they'd arrived together. It just made me wonder if they'd spent the entire day together, and if that was the case, did it mean Alec wasn't over his ex?

As I watched, he scanned the crowd, his gaze stopping when it found me. He took a step in my direction, and I realized that I really didn't want to have a conversation with him and Keli in such a public environment, especially since I didn't know what had happened after I'd left this morning. I couldn't imagine Keli being okay with seeing me come out of Alec's room or Evanne's enthusiastic greeting. I didn't even want to consider how she was taking his clear determination to get to me.

"Excuse me," I said to Mr. Buchannan with a smile. "I need to go find Siobhan before the meeting starts."

I cut around Mr. Buchannan and walked through the crowd as if I had a specific destination in mind. I'd seen Siobhan over here, but if I couldn't find her quickly, there were plenty of other people around. Pretty much the only person I wanted to talk to less than Alec right now would be Vice Principal Harvey.

I'd even take a conversation with Mrs. Crenshaw at the moment.

Fortunately, I didn't need to resort to such drastic measures. Siobhan and I talked for a few minutes as I stayed out of sight behind a decorative planter, and then Principal McKenna called the meeting to order.

I risked a look around as people moved to find seats and saw that Alec and Keli were sitting a few rows away. He didn't look happy, but I told myself that it wasn't my problem. I wasn't here for him. I was here to talk about keeping everyone at Kurt Wright safe.

By the time Principal McKenna closed down the official meeting more than two hours later and invited anyone who wished to discuss things further to remain, I'd had enough. With so many wealthy and connected families, putting new security measures into place should have been easy, but most of the meeting had been spent in second amendment debates, as if this was the time or the place for politics.

We had a chance to make our school safer, and all anyone cared about was being one hundred percent right. No one was willing to get off their high horse and offer a compromise that both sides could get behind. Despite not wanting to draw attention to myself, I'd even tried suggesting that we try something on a short-term basis and then reassess at a later date to see if it'd helped.

The snort of derision had come from the direction of Mrs. Crenshaw, but she hadn't been alone in her scorn of my idea. Others were just a little more polite, choosing to smile condescendingly as they'd told me that when I was older and understood how these things worked, I'd know why that wasn't feasible.

I'd kept my mouth shut through the rest of the meeting, and as soon as Principal McKenna said it was over, I was on my feet and heading for the door. I'd probably get reprimanded for leaving so quickly, but I'd felt Alec's eyes on me the entire time. I needed to get out before he caught up with me.

I should have known better than to lose track of my surroundings.

In my rush to get away from Alec, I practically ran through an open door and smacked face-first into someone who smelled like cigarettes and too much cheap cologne.

Shit.

"Whoa there, Lumen. Where do you think you're going?" Cornelius Harvey's hands closed around my upper arms, and he moved me a step to the side.

It wasn't far enough.

And he didn't let go.

"I'm leaving, Vice Principal Harvey," I said with the best smile I could muster. "I've got a really bad headache."

"Is that so?" He released one of my arms only to pat my cheek. "Come on, we can get you something to cure that hangover."

My jaw dropped. "I don't have a hangover. I have a *headache*."

"Sure you do." He winked at me. "How about you let me get my coat, and I'll take you home. I'll show you what these magic fingers can do."

I wasn't hungover, but I was starting to suspect that his overpowering cologne was to cover up the fact that he was drunk. I took a step back and managed to pull my arm free. "Thank you for the offer, but I'm fine to get home on my own, and my roommate will take care of me."

His expression darkened. "Is that how your parents taught you to thank someone who offered to help you?"

If I hadn't already known he was one of those sleaze-bags who thought buying a woman dinner meant she owed him a sexual favor as repayment or gratitude, that comment would've made it clear.

"I'm going to go now." I went to step around him, and he grabbed my arm again. I stiffened and met his gaze full on. "Let me go."

"Don't forget," he said, eyes narrowing, "I'm your boss. You should think carefully before you speak out of turn, or you might find your contract not being renewed come spring."

How the hell had this asshole ended up second-in-command at a school?

I didn't have time to consider the answer to my question because someone grabbed Harvey from the other side and jerked him around. I heard knuckles hit flesh, and then Harvey dropped to the ground, revealing my savior to be none other than Alec.

The fury on Alec's face was like nothing I'd ever seen before, and every ounce of it was directed at Harvey.

"If I ever hear of you harassing Lumen or any other woman, for that matter, you're going to be answering to me." His voice was even, his words clipped and precise as he maintained control. He clearly wanted to make sure Harvey understood everything he said. "Believe me when I say that you will not find that a pleasant experience."

I was still staring at Alec, mouth hanging open in shock when Keli came running up behind him.

"Alec! Are you okay?" She grabbed his hand. "It was so brave of you to defend *Evanne's teacher* like that. Did you see that, sweetie?" She looked down at Evanne. "Your daddy is such a good man, sticking up for your *teacher* like that."

I'd had enough. I appreciated Alec's gesture, especially since it meant I didn't need to try to explain to Principal McKenna why I'd kneed the vice principal in the nuts, but that didn't mean I wanted to stick around to hear Keli fawning all over him.

It had nothing to do with the emphasis she kept putting on the fact that I was Evanne's teacher, like she didn't know that Alec and I'd spent the night together last night. I would've preferred she came out and said what she really thought of me instead of that underhanded shit too many people pulled.

NINETEEN
ALEC

I yanked my hand away from Keli and stuck both of my hands in my pockets to remind myself that it wouldn't be smart to punch the bastard again. I'd seen red when he'd threatened Lumen, and that slip of control might end up costing me, but my gut said this arsehole was a coward, and he wouldn't want to have to explain to anyone the reason why I'd hit him.

I looked away from the man sluggishly getting to his feet and saw that Lumen was gone.

"*Shite*," I cursed under my breath. I needed to talk to her now more than ever. In addition to wanting to explain about our unexpected visit this morning, I wanted to know how long this *clot-heid* had been harassing her.

"Daddy, what happened?" Evanne's voice brought me back to myself.

"What was that, *mo chride*?" I looked down at her.

Her eyes were huge, but she didn't look upset. "What happened?"

The vice principal was limping away now, shooting furtive little glances over his shoulder. Fortunately for me, the entire incident had taken place in a shadowed alcove just out of the main traffic area, so it didn't appear to have raised any alarms. If Harvey was smart, he'd claim he fell on his own, and if anyone had seen anything, they'd assume that was what had happened.

"What did you see?" I kept my tone casual, but whatever half-truth I told would have to be based on what Evanne had seen with her own eyes. I wouldn't tell her I hadn't done something if she'd seen me do it.

"Mr. Harvey on the ground and Ms. Browne looking weird."

I gave Evanne a crooked smile. "Mr. Harvey must have tripped on something and surprised Ms. Browne."

"Don't be modest, Alec," Keli said, wrapping her arms around me. "Evanne should know what a brave man her daddy is."

"Keli." I gritted my teeth. "No."

She gave me the same patronizing smile she'd always given me right before she announced how foolish I was.

"Mr. Harvey and Ms. Browne were talking," Keli said, looking down at Evanne. "And Mr. Harvey must have said something mean because your daddy told him that wasn't right."

"And then he tripped?"

Keli leaned into me. "Yes, sweetie. Then he tripped."

What was she playing at? She could have told Evanne that I'd punched the vice principal and hoped that it would make Evanne upset with me, or even afraid of me. She could have drawn attention to the situation and made people question exactly why I'd been so quick to defend a teacher I supposedly didn't know.

When I'd stepped away from the kiss she'd planted on me this morning, I had fully expected retaliation of some kind. She'd remained at the house all day, and I'd waited for the other shoe to drop. Then she'd announced that she was coming to the meeting with Evanne and me, and I'd thought she would perhaps say something in front of the principal. Instead, she'd been quiet and pleasant.

Things between us had never been acrimonious, but this was *too* nice.

Something was going to come back to bite me in the ass.

"Daddy." Evanne tugged on the arm Keli wasn't currently hanging on. "Can Mommy sleep over tonight?

She said she'd take me to a movie tomorrow, and this way, she could be there when I wake up."

How was I supposed to say no to that?

"All right, *mo chride*. But you still have to get your homework done before you can go to the movie."

"Okay." She beamed at me. "Mommy can help me."

That was something positive, at least.

Besides, it wasn't as if I'd be having sex with Keli. She'd stay in a perfectly acceptable guest room next to Evanne, and it would make Evanne happy. That was all that mattered.

I'd figure out things with Lumen later.

TWENTY

LUMEN

THE SECOND TIME IT HAPPENED, I HAD TO ADMIT that it wasn't my imagination. They were talking about me.

When I hadn't gotten a call or a visit from Principal McKenna or the police, I'd hoped that meant Harvey had decided not to make an issue of what'd happened. He'd probably been embarrassed, but since Alec had been the one who'd thrown the punch, Harvey might have decided that it'd be in his best interest to let it go. He had, after all, been the one to tell me just how important Alec McCrae was to the school.

Still, I'd been nervous when I'd gotten up this morning. Even if Harvey didn't go to any authorities about what'd happened, that didn't mean he'd leave me alone. Some people might've been intimidated by Alec's threat, and I didn't doubt Harvey would leave me alone any time Alec was around, but I'd known men like Cornelius Harvey my whole life, and I didn't doubt for a moment that he'd go after me even harder as vengeance for his humiliation.

My plan was to make sure I wasn't alone with him and avoid the situation altogether. I didn't like the idea of having to essentially hide from him, but my options were fairly limited, and this offered the best solution, no matter how much it sucked. The entire time I was on the bus, I was making mental lists. Lists about the things I could do in the office when I had free time, the teachers who I could make excuses to walk with, the parents I could count on to drop off their kids early or pick them up late.

The moment I walked into the building, however, I knew it wouldn't be that easy. Standing at the door of Mr. Yu's fifth-grade classroom was junior high science teacher Mrs. Rogers, both of them looking guilty as they glanced at me. I didn't have to ask what they'd been talking about. It was written all over their faces. The disapproval. The suspicion.

Someone had been talking about me, and my gut said it was Vice Principal Harvey.

I didn't yet know if he'd been talking about what had happened with Alec or if he was simply running his mouth about the sort of woman I was. Maybe laying the groundwork for discrediting me if I accused him of anything. Maybe just wanting to be a bastard because I'd turned him down and arrogant assholes like him rarely took rejection well. Maybe there was a third reason I wasn't seeing yet.

No matter what his reasoning was, it was going to give me more than a headache.

"Morning," I said with a tight smile. They muttered the same in return but couldn't meet my eyes. I pretended I didn't care. It wasn't like we'd been on our way to being friends or anything like that.

"He told Principal McKenna that he tripped over a rock that'd fallen out of a flowerbed."

Adrian Lyons was the high school chemistry teacher here, and I was fairly certain that he'd taught Adam and Eve. He insisted that all the teachers call him by his first name, and despite his age, he was as sharp as they came. If anyone could see through Harvey's lies, it'd be him.

"If you ask me, that's a load of crap. Landed on his face and on his butt at the same time, apparently." Adrian didn't even bother trying to keep his voice down.

I liked him.

"What do you think happened?" Siobhan asked. She looked at me and then her eyes slid away.

She'd heard something too. Great.

"I think he was hitting the bottle before the meeting and fell down more than once," Adrian said. "He always smells like that nasty mouth wash. What's it called? Listerine?"

"Do you think Principal McKenna suspects that too?" Siobhan asked.

I passed by before I could hear Adrian's response. Each step closer to the office I got, the more my stomach twisted and clenched. When I finally passed Alice, I wondered if I should have called in sick. I'd probably throw up at some point in the near future so it wouldn't have totally been a lie. At least she didn't look at me strangely. That could, however, have been because she was on the phone. Still, I'd take it.

Then, as I picked up my mail, I heard Alice say something that made me feel like I'd gotten a firing squad reprieve.

"No, Vice Principal Harvey is out today with a back injury. After he goes to the doctor today, he'll have a better idea of when he should be back in. He just stopped in to get his mail this morning."

I closed my eyes. It was only one day, but it would at least get me a better idea of what everyone else thought. Once school was out, I'd start trying to figure out what to do next.

DESPITE KNOWING that Harvey had taken the day off, I spent the next several hours with nerves stretched tight enough to snap. Every time I stepped out of my classroom or my door opened, I found myself tensing, waiting for Principal McKenna to show up and inform me that I'd been fired. By the time the kids were getting antsy for the final bell to ring, I was exhausted and watching the clock as intently as they were.

"All right," I said, calling the students' attention from their worksheets. "Pass your worksheets forward, and you may talk quietly until the bell rings."

I walked along the first row, picking up the papers as I went. Today was Evanne's day to sit in the front, and hers was the last desk I got to. Because of how full I'd kept the day's schedule, I hadn't had much time to have a conversation with her about what she'd seen or heard Saturday evening. Honestly, I'd been afraid of what she might say, but as I took her row's papers from her, I told myself to stop being a jerk and talk to the kid.

"Did you have a good day yesterday?"

The smile that lit up her face made anything she might say worth it.

"I did! Mommy had a sleepover!"

My smile froze. Hell, *everything* in me froze. "She did?"

"Mm-hm." Evanne leaned forward in her seat. "She read me a story, and then when I got up yesterday, we had breakfast together, the three of us."

And that answered the question as to whether or not the sleepover had been because Alec had needed to go on some emergency trip or something.

Evanne kept going. "Then we did a fashion show and watched a movie and played with my robots."

"It sounds like you had fun," I said woodenly. I wanted to ask if Keli had spent the night again last night, but that would've been completely inappropriate.

And I wasn't sure I wanted to know the answer to that question.

"Now that Mommy's back from her trip, there's all sorts of things she said we can do together. She wants me to write them down."

As Evanne started listing all the things that she wanted to do with Keli now that they'd been reunited, I couldn't help but wonder if this meant Keli was back permanently. If so, would that mean Alec and she would go back to their original custody arrangement? If they did, I assumed that would mean Keli would be the one taking care of Evanne's school things. I didn't like the idea of having to see her numerous times throughout the year, but the positive side to that would be that my time with Alec could be separated from time with Evanne.

Except I didn't know what Keli's return meant for her relationship with Alec. Things didn't seem to be going back the way they had been, at least not based on what Alec had told me of their relationship. He and Keli hadn't done anything together with Evanne, barely interacting with each other at all. Which begged the question, did that mean Keli was trying to become a bigger part of Alec's life too? And if that was the case, where did it leave me?

Too. Fucking. Confusing.

The bell rang, breaking me from my thoughts. The kids scattered as they always did. Some preferred to talk to their friends until their rides got here, and only then would they get their things and put on their coats. Others knew their parents, or drivers, or nannies were already waiting and went straight to the coatrack to gather their things. A couple of the students changed what they did from day-to-day.

Evanne was one of those, and today, she wanted to talk to me.

Any other time, I would've been thrilled to spend some one-on-one time with any of my students, even the ones who acted up in class. I was a firm believer in establishing a rapport with students in casual conversations that weren't dependent on asking and answering questions. Plus, I genuinely enjoyed talking to Evanne.

I just wasn't sure how much more I could fake being excited about all the things Keli and Evanne were going to do together, and that just made me feel like shit because I should have been happy that Evanne was excited to be spending time with her mom. Instead, I was wallowing because I didn't know where I fit in that world anymore.

If I fit.

"Mommy!" Evanne squealed as she took off toward the door. "You came!"

I turned, a polite smile on my face. My jealousy wasn't her fault. I was Evanne's teacher first. She had to take precedence. I couldn't ever forget that. Not even when Keli gave me a smug as fuck look as Evanne hugged her.

I just needed to know if that look was only about Evanne's excitement over seeing her...or if it was her way of telling me that she was back in Alec's life too.

TWENTY-ONE
ALEC

Dammit!

Thanks to two red lights, I was ten minutes later in getting to the school than I'd wanted to be, which meant I was there five minutes after school let out for the day instead of five minutes before. In my head, I knew it wasn't the end of the world. Kids were sometimes at the school up to fifteen or twenty minutes after the end of the day, but those other kids weren't my responsibility. They weren't *my* kid.

The parking lot wasn't full when I pulled into a spot, but it also wasn't completely empty. The parents and staff I passed all had the same pinched, harried expression, and I wondered if I looked the same. I hated when I got off schedule, when the control I needed slipped through my fingers.

My shoes squeaked on the tile floor as I made my way down the hall to Evanne's classroom. I'd passed two teachers before I realized that they were giving me sideways looks, and not the usual admiration I received when I went places where the money I spent made a difference.

I suddenly realized the most likely reason they were watching me.

Shite.

I may not have heard from the police or from a lawyer, but that didn't necessarily mean Cornelius Harvey had kept our encounter a secret. Or, also a possibility, someone had seen at least a portion of the altercation but didn't know the facts.

I didn't know which would be the better of the two possibilities.

Not that either of them would be too problematic. I had excellent lawyers and a defensible reason for what I'd done. Even without a law degree, I could think of half a dozen ways I would come out on top. I just preferred to not have to deal with the headache it'd cause.

Lumen was by her desk, gathering up her things when I stepped into her room. A quick scan around the room said she was alone.

"Where's my daughter?"

Lumen spun around, her hand going to her chest.

"Dammit, Alec! You scared me." Then she frowned. "What are you doing here?"

That single question struck fear into me. "What do you mean? Where is Evanne?"

She looked puzzled rather than worried, which calmed me some, because if she thought Evanne was missing, she wouldn't have been so calm. Still, I needed her to answer my question.

"Evanne's mother picked her up several minutes ago."

I clenched my teeth. "I didn't know."

"Keli Miller is still on the approved list for drop-offs and pick-ups," Lumen said. "If you wish to change that, you do it at the office."

It was my turn to frown. Her tone when I'd first startled her had been genuine. Now, she sounded stiff. "Keli is Evanne's mother. Why would I want to remove her from the list?"

"No reason. I just wanted to make sure you knew the proper procedure." Lumen's smile was tight and didn't reach her eyes.

I didn't like it, but I had a more important question to ask. "Did she happen to say where they were going?"

She shook her head, and her expression didn't change. "We didn't speak." I waited for her to add to her statement. After a long pause, she lifted an eyebrow. "Was there anything else you needed?"

I sighed and rubbed my forehead. My head had begun to pound the moment I'd realized I'd be late, and with every additional frustration, my headache had only grown. Clearly, Lumen was pissed about something. Considering the way her colleagues had looked at me, I had a feeling I knew why she was upset. My rash actions Saturday evening had consequences that not only affected me but Lumen as well. I'd give her some time while I reached out to Keli and found out what the hell was going on. Then, once Lumen was ready to talk, we'd do just that.

Until then, I had things to do. "I'll be going now."

Frustration twisted my gut as she ignored me, and my temper spiked. Without another word, I turned and stalked away. I had too many fucking women in my life.

As soon as I started the car, I used Bluetooth to call Keli, but she didn't answer. In fact, it went straight to voicemail.

"Keli." I struggled to keep my voice even in case she listened to the voicemail on speaker, and Evanne was nearby. "I don't mind that you picked up Evanne, but I need you to let me know when you do that. I'm going back to the house. If you're not there, please let me know where you two are and when you and Evanne will return."

I waited until I ended the call before I swore again. Keli had done stupid shit before, but it'd only ever been mildly annoying. What had been happening since she'd returned from Italy was too much. She and I were long overdue for a talk.

The moment I opened the door, Evanne flew into my arms, chattering a mile a minute about how she and Keli were making pizza for dinner. I masked my relief with a kiss to Evanne's forehead and carried her into the kitchen. The guilty expression that flashed across Keli's face the moment she saw me was proof enough for me that she'd heard my voicemail, but I didn't immediately accuse her of anything. Evanne wasn't going to be present for the discussion her mother and I needed to have.

"The pizza's ready to go in the oven," she said, her eyes on Evanne. "Why don't you start on your home-work, and your dad and I will clean up, okay?"

"Can I do it in front of the TV?" Evanne looked at me for permission.

"*May*," I corrected.

"*May* I do my homework in front of the television?" she asked, the corners of her mouth tipping up in a grin.

"Aye, since you helped with dinner, you may."

"Yay!" She ran toward the living room full tilt, and I couldn't bring myself to remind her to slow down. With everything that had happened at the school and Keli returning, Evanne and my plan to run together had fallen by the wayside.

This needed to stop. Evanne had to come first.

"Keli, we need to talk."

"I'm sorry I didn't tell you I was going to pick Evanne up today," she rushed to say. "This past week, I've been trying to get back into my routine, and today I realized why it's been so difficult. Taking Evanne to and from school has always been a part of my day during the school year. Without it, I felt like I was off."

She stepped closer to me and put her hand on my arm, reminding me of how she'd kissed me on Saturday. Once I'd gotten past the initial shock, I'd stepped back and simply said *no*, but I hadn't addressed it with anything more than that. In fact, I'd intentionally *not* been thinking about it...or about what she'd said right before.

"I just wanted things to get back to normal," she said.

"You coming here to make dinner with Evanne is a pretty far cry from normal," I pointed out.

Cherry red lips curved up in what had once been a sensual smile. Now, all that served was to remind me of another woman's smile, one without ulterior motives.

"It doesn't have to be." Her hand slid up my forearm. "I meant what I said on Saturday. I want us to have a second chance."

I picked up her hand and removed it from my arm, struggling to find the right balance between firm and gentle. "That's not only your decision to make."

"I know," she immediately agreed. "But I was the one who walked away before, and I just wanted you to know that I regret it. I'm not going anywhere this time. I want us to work."

I had so many responses going through my mind, I didn't know where to start.

She had ended things between us, but it had been more complicated than her statement implied. Before she'd told me she was pregnant, I'd wanted to end the relationship because it had been obvious to me that we hadn't been compatible, but once I'd learned about the baby, I'd pushed those thoughts back, not knowing if a child would change things. A few months after Evanne was born, Keli had broken up with me, saying she wanted more from the relationship than I could give her.

She'd been right. Especially back then. I'd been twenty-five, and she'd been twenty when Evanne had been born. We'd both changed since then.

Which meant I couldn't ignore what she was saying simply because it hadn't worked before.

Except I wasn't attracted to Keli anymore. I hadn't been for a long time. Not physically, and I didn't find her personality appealing either. Even if I hadn't been interested in Lumen, I wouldn't have immediately agreed to what Keli wanted.

But I couldn't completely discount Lumen either.

I wanted her more than I'd ever wanted a woman, and not only for the physical reasons. I liked her as a person and enjoyed the time we spent together. I'd already let her closer than Keli had ever been. I didn't want to give Lumen up.

But Keli was Evanne's mother.

I'd been eight years old when my mother died, and it had devastated all of us. Even all these years later, the pain was still there. While I had eventually accepted Theresa and her children as part of the family, it hadn't been easy. It had actually been the birth of the twins, Sean and Xander, who had finally brought both sides together to form a whole. Still, I struggled with how to balance missing my mother and loving my family as it was now.

I didn't want Evanne to go through that. I didn't want her to worry that accepting a stepmother would be a betrayal of Keli. I didn't want her to feel that her loyalty and love had to be unevenly divided or that she needed to protect her mother from her feelings toward another mother figure.

Before Evanne, I hadn't really thought about having a family, but after learning that I would be a father, the immediate vision I'd had in my head had been of a child with both of their biological parents being there for them their entire lives.

I'd already fucked that up once by not being able to give Keli what she'd needed in order to stay back then. We'd made things work with what we'd had, but now I had a chance to give Evanne both of her parents, together.

Because of Lumen, I couldn't flat-out accept it, but because of Evanne, I couldn't refuse it either. I needed the one thing I knew I didn't have much of.

Time.

"I need to think about it. We can talk more after Evanne goes to bed."

TWENTY-TWO

LUMEN

I really needed to get a car.

This wasn't the first time I'd had that thought recently, but it was becoming more frequent. Besides the difficulties that came with taking the bus to get to work – I wasn't looking forward to the evenings I had projects to take home – I had a feeling I would be the person Soleil called when she needed something that she didn't want Brie or Josalyn to know about.

Such as getting caught shoplifting at the Grab 'N Go two blocks from the group home.

I'd just finished washing up from dinner when store security called to say that my 'sister,' Soleil, had been seen stealing, and they were now holding her. If I was willing to come down and get her, we could discuss whether or not to call the cops.

Despite the little white lie concerning our relationship, I was glad that she'd given my name, though I wished the circumstances had been different. She still hadn't told me why she'd called me the day of the shooting, but I didn't think whatever that had been was resolved. She'd been looking more tired lately, and the few times I'd caught an unguarded glimpse of her eyes, they'd been haunted. Something was going on but pushing would only make her retreat more. I had to take things at her speed, no matter how maddening it was.

It was drizzling when I got off the bus, so I put up my umbrella and started up the sidewalk. Since the store was only a block from the bus station, it wasn't long before I was shaking off my umbrella and stepping inside, grateful for the rush of warm air that greeted me. I went straight for the back where the security guard had told me he'd be waiting with Soleil.

The door was open, but I knocked anyway. Soleil was sitting on one side of a desk, her head down, shoulders slumped. She didn't even look up when I stepped inside or when the man on the other side of the desk stood up. He was older, probably working this as a semi-retirement or retirement job, but the way he held himself made me think he'd been a cop or something similar.

"Lumen Browne," I said as I held out my hand. "Thank you for calling me."

"I'm Malone." His grip was firm but not tight. He gestured to the seat next to Soleil. "The store gives me discretion when it comes to how shoplifting is handled, and for anyone underage, I like to get a family member's thoughts on the subject before deciding what to do."

The look he gave me said he wasn't so sure that Soleil and I were related, but he didn't ask. With as many blended families as there were out there, Soleil and my obvious physical differences didn't necessarily exclude us from being siblings. I had a feeling that, rather than embarrass anyone by asking, he planned to wait to see what I had to say.

"What did you take?" I asked Soleil directly.

She shrugged and didn't look at me.

"Malone?" I turned my question to him.

He hesitated, and then said, "I'd rather she told you herself. It doesn't need to be now. I'll just say that it wasn't expensive, and it can go back on the shelf, so if this isn't a habit, I'd be willing to let her go with a stern warning."

Something was off here. The last thing I'd expected was security to want to go easy on her and to not tell me what it was she'd stolen. I met his gaze, surprised to find concern there.

"I have a granddaughter about her age," he said. "Sometimes, kids do things without thinking them through, and a second chance serves them better than harsher consequences."

Soleil shifted in her chair, but when I glanced her way, she still wouldn't look at me.

"I'll take her home now," I said. She stood when I stood. "Thank him, Soleil. A lot of places would've called the cops first."

I wasn't actually her sister or anyone with any authority over her, but she'd wanted me to come help her, and I was counting on that to get her to express some gratitude.

"Thank you," she muttered.

"Let this be the last time you're in this situation," he said before turning to me. "I just need a signature here saying I released her into your custody."

I signed, and then we left. There wasn't another bus stop between here and the group home, which meant we were going to walk. With only one umbrella, her choices were limited. She could walk close enough to stay dry, or she could be stubborn and get even wetter and more miserable by the time we reached the house. At first, I thought she'd choose the latter, but she didn't. When we reached the sidewalk, I asked the question that had been burning in my mind.

"What did you take?"

She didn't say anything, and I let the question hang

between us. It had to be her choice, but what she chose would determine what I told Brie, and she'd been in the system long enough to know what that would mean. Placing teenagers in foster homes was difficult enough. Kids with run-ins with the law were nearly impossible. She had to decide that it would be better to trust me and hope I agreed not to say anything to Brie or Josalyn than it would be to keep her mouth shut and hope for the same.

We went a block before she spoke, her voice low enough that I almost missed it.

And I was immediately glad I hadn't.

"It was a pregnancy test."

It took me a few seconds to shut down my automatic response of shock. "Is this...preemptive? Do you want to have it because you're planning to have sex with someone, and you'd feel better having it just in case?"

She shook her head but didn't say anything else.

"Is your period late or are you scared because you recently had unprotected sex?"

Instead of an answer, I got a question. "Are you going to tell?"

A bright fluorescent light to my right caught my eye, and I saw an opportunity to give me time to think before I answered. "Well, first we need to know if there's anything to tell." I gestured to the pharmacy we were next to. "The way I see it, trying to pocket a ten-dollar test isn't really the issue. Come on."

She followed me into the parking lot and then through the pharmacy to the appropriate aisle. I picked up one box, read the back, then chose another one. After we went through the checkout, I snagged Soleil's sleeve and steered her toward the bathrooms.

"I want you to take it now," I said. When she glared at me, I gave her a steady look right back. "I mean it, Soleil. I need to have all the information before I decide anything else."

For a moment, I thought she'd storm off, but after a few seconds, she grabbed the test and went into the bathroom. I gave her a minute before I followed. I doubted she wanted to wait alone, but I also doubted she'd ask for me to wait with her. If she told me to leave, I would, but I didn't want her to go through it alone.

"It's just me," I said quietly. "I'm going to wait out here."

I leaned back on the counter and did just that. I wasn't sure if she planned to wait the whole time in the stall or not, but she came out of the stall half a minute later. She set the white stick on the counter and washed her hands, head ducked so her hair hid her face. After she dried her hands, she paced, lips moving as if she was counting her steps. I kept an eye on my watch, and when I straightened, she stopped, knowing it was time.

"Can you...?" Her bottom lip trembled, and my heart broke for her.

I nodded and looked at the test. A rush of relief went through me. "It's negative."

She put out her hand and caught the edge on the counter. "What...what are the chances it's wrong?"

"They're fairly accurate," I said. "And if anything, they give false positives, not negatives."

Soleil closed her eyes for a few seconds, and I took care of the test. After I washed my hands, I put my hand on her shoulder and squeezed.

"I'll wait just outside."

She nodded to let me know that she understood, and then I left. I waited until I was a few steps away, with my back to the door, before I dropped control, letting chaos reign now so I could get my head together when Soleil needed me.

Why did the girl think she was pregnant?

By who?

Was it one of the guys from the home?

I should get condoms, maybe talk to her about birth control.

Was she having regular sex?

Where?

My thoughts were interrupted by a text alert. I pulled my phone from my purse, smiling when I saw Alec's name. I opened the message, and my stomach fell.

Things have changed now that Keli is back. You and I need to take a break while I figure out what's going on with my family. Evanne's well-being has to come first.

I'd known this was coming. There'd been plenty of evidence pointing toward it, and I'd even warned myself.

The bathroom door opened, and I shoved all my feelings down into a box. I'd learned to do it at a young age, and it was something I still employed when it was necessary. Like now.

Completely understandable.

I sent it and put my phone back in my purse. Soleil had to come first with me. Heaven knew she wouldn't come first with anyone else. It wasn't Brie's or Josalyn's fault. They had too many people to take care of and not enough time or resources to do it to the best of their abilities.

"Ready?" I asked with a smile.

She nodded, and we headed for the door.

I needed to find out who Soleil had had sex with. One of the boys at the house would be bad. A kid at her school wouldn't be great. In fact, there was a good chance that, no matter who it was, it'd be illegal. She was fourteen.

I wouldn't say anything to Brie or Josalyn just yet. I wanted to get more information before I did that. Soleil wouldn't tell them anything, and once I crossed that line to give them information, she might not talk to me either. I had to know more first.

And until then, I'd protect Soleil myself.

TWENTY-THREE

ALEC

COMPLETELY UNDERSTANDABLE.

Lumen had sent me that text last night in response to me saying we needed time apart. No disagreement. No asking about what it meant or how long I thought I might need.

I should have been thankful that she hadn't become angry or accused me of leading her on or using her. Neither of those things were true, but someone who was hurt might not be thinking clearly. What I feared, however, was that Lumen had been able to think clearly because she wasn't hurt.

It was unfair of me, I knew. I'd changed the expectations between us the first time. I'd told her that I'd wanted to pursue something with her. I'd given her a key to my house.

And then I'd blown it all up because Keli had decided she wanted us to be a family.

I told myself I had done it the right way. When I'd realized that I needed to at least try to make a normal family for Evanne, I had been honest with Lumen rather than keeping her in the dark. I'd been as polite and matter-of-fact as I could. There wasn't anything more I could have done.

Completely understandable.

So formal. As if she was simply talking to the father of one of her students and not a man who had been her first lover.

Except the father of a student *was* all that I was anymore. Judging by the lack of emotion in Lumen's response, it was likely all that I would ever be, no matter what came of Keli's and my attempt to make a stable home for our daughter.

Lumen wouldn't wait for me. I had been tempted to ask her to, but it wouldn't have been fair. That didn't stop a part of me from being hurt that she hadn't offered or told me to take all the time I needed.

Perhaps that would be for the best. I would have felt guilty trying to make a family for Evanne while knowing Lumen had put her life on hold. This way, she was free to meet other men, go on dates...take other lovers.

The jealousy that burned through me hurt more

than I liked, but I assured myself it was only natural. It would go away soon enough.

"Hey, honey." Keli's hands landed on my shoulders. "Dinner's almost ready."

My natural instinct was to shrug off her touch, but I kept it back. I had agreed to give this an honest try and refusing to have any contact with her wouldn't be holding my word. That didn't, however, mean that I had to encourage it either. Ignoring appeared to be the best middle ground.

"Thank you, Keli. I'll be right there."

I breathed a sigh of relief when she left. She and I hadn't spent this much time together even when we had dated. Yesterday, she hadn't left until I'd said that I needed to go to bed, and I'd gotten the impression that she would have offered to go with me if she'd gotten the slightest hint of encouragement. Then today, she'd picked up Evanne after school – remembering to let me know at least – and had been here when I'd gotten home from work.

One positive out of it, at least, was that I hadn't needed to help Evanne with her homework. Keli had also taken over reading to our daughter last night. It almost seemed like Keli had taken the routine she and Evanne once had before the custody change and had simply applied it here. In a way, that was good because routine was important, particularly during the school year. I knew all too well what it was like to have one's world shaken and turned upside-down as a child.

The reminder strengthened my resolve, and I left my laptop on the table next to my chair and headed into the kitchen. The table was set, and the last of the food was coming out of the oven as Evanne jumped up from her seat to come over and give me a hug.

"No pizza today," she said. "But Mommy said if I'm good, we can have pizza tomorrow."

I added that to my mental list of things to talk about after Evanne went to bed. We needed to figure out a way for both of us to be involved in decisions that affected either Evanne or all of us directly, even something as simple as dinner. When Keli had made the unilateral decision to sign over primary custody to me and leave the country, she'd lost the right to go back to being the one responsible for all the decisions regarding our daughter. Whether Keli liked it or not, I would no longer defer to her judgment automatically.

"What are we having tonight then, *mo chride*?" I asked before planting a kiss on the top of Evanne's head.

"Tuna casserole." She made a face, but it vanished the moment Keli turned toward us.

I watched Evanne go to her usual seat and wondered if Keli knew that Evanne didn't like tuna casserole but expected her to eat it for whatever reason, or if Evanne hadn't told her mother because she thought any sort of disagreement or negative expression would send Keli away. I needed to find a way to reassure Evanne that it wasn't her responsibility to make Keli happy, and if Keli left again, it wouldn't be due to anything the little girl had done.

Dinner was pleasant enough. We made polite conversation, punctuated by Keli's stories and her new plan about how to become the world's fastest eight-year-old.

"Ms. Browne says that when we want to do something, we should write down what we need to do it and then figure out how," Evanne said.

My stomach tightened at the name. I'd been expecting it. Even if Evanne didn't understand relationship dynamics, Lumen was still her teacher and one about whom Evanne cared and admired. I couldn't ask her to not talk about her teacher.

"Really?" Keli raised her eyebrows. "I think that's a bit hard for third-graders. Shouldn't she be teaching you about multiplication and Christopher Columbus discovering America? That sort of thing?"

"Christopher Columbus didn't discover America, Mom." Evanne shook her head. "Ms. Browne told us about..."

The rest of this school year would be like this, I realized. Even if Keli took over all school activities and meetings, I wouldn't be free of reminders until June. I could only hope that Keli being here would keep Evanne from asking why Lumen hadn't come over in a while. That was a conversation I dreaded.

"...and then she said that whenever we read anything in history, we need to remember that nobody's perfect and every country has done bad things to someone at some point."

"Oh, is that what she said?" Keli's voice was tight, displeasure written on her face. "Did she say why she was telling you that?"

Evanne nodded, expression solemn. "Because we can't change the past, but we can change the future. She said that even us kids can do it by being nice to people and helping people who need it. Like donating toys and clothes to kids to don't have them."

"She wants you to give away your toys and clothes?" Keli looked at me, her eyes comically wide. "Did you hear that, Alec? Evanne's teacher is telling her to give away all of her toys and clothes. Then who has to replace them? Us."

It was on the tip of my tongue to remind her that I was the one who actually paid for all of Evanne's things, whether through child support or actual purchases. I didn't mind doing it, but Keli's righteous indignation wasn't easy to stomach.

"Not all of them, Mommy," Evanne cut in. "The ones I don't play with anymore. Or clothes I outgrew. We're going to have a drive in November, and I'm going to give away my toys because I'll have new ones from my birthday."

"That's very generous of you, *mo chride*." I smiled at her. "We'll have to put on the calendar a day when we can go through your things and decide what you're going to give away and what you want to keep."

"Alec, do you really think that's appropriate?"

I stifled a frown. "There's nothing inappropriate about helping the less fortunate."

"It is when a teacher is telling the kids they have to do it just because their parents have money. I didn't realize Kurt Wright encouraged *handouts*."

She said the word like it was distasteful, and I knew her issue wasn't with what Lumen had taught the kids but rather who Lumen was to me.

Had been to me.

"Alec—"

"Keli." Her name held a warning, and for a brief moment, I caught a glimpse of something angry. Rather than getting into an argument in front of Evanne, I deflected by asking a question. "When you first looked into the school for Evanne, did you research social and political views?"

In addition to moving the conversation along, the question also served as a reminder that Keli had been the one to choose the school. If she didn't agree with their curriculum, the responsibility lay with her.

"It just makes me wonder how closely the principal monitors what his teachers say." Keli drained the last of her wine. "I can't be the only parent who has a problem with it...unless Ms. Browne used all of the parent-teacher meetings to charm the fathers like she did you."

"Ms. Browne and I met prior to the start of school." It took work not to spit the words out. "Neither of us knew who the other was until the second week of school."

"I'm done," Evanne announced.

"Your homework is done?" I asked, grateful for the change of subject.

"Yes."

"Go brush your teeth and get ready for bed."

"Daddy, will you read to me tonight? Mommy doesn't do the voices right for *Katie Morag*."

"Of course, *mo chride*." I smiled as she skipped off toward her room.

"I swear you bought her that Scottish book just because you knew I couldn't do the accent." Keli poured herself another glass of wine and then held out the bottle to me.

"No, thank you." I had a bottle of Scotch with my name on it for after Keli left.

"Suit yourself," she said as she took a long drink. "Now, how about you tell me how you met Evanne's teacher, if it wasn't at school."

Shit.

"I don't see why that's important." I kept my voice mild.

"Maybe because I have a right to know more about the woman you had sleepovers with...in the same house where our daughter was sleeping." Keli's eyes narrowed. "I seem to recall you grilling me about every man I've dated since you."

"You're right," I agreed, "but you already know that Lumen is an elementary teacher and that the relationship is over. Why does it matter where I met her?"

"Why are you being so evasive?" she shot back. "Did you pick her up in some skeezy sex club or something?"

I sighed and pinched the bridge of my nose. "Lumen and I are done, Keli. Just let it go."

"Daddy! I'm ready!"

I stood up, and Keli grabbed my hand.

"Tell me, or I'll ask her myself."

I didn't doubt for a second she'd do just that, and I

could picture how completely mortified Lumen would be, how she wouldn't know how much to say.

"I had a bad day and couldn't relax, so I went to a massage parlor to have my back worked on. Lumen was the masseuse. A week later, I went to MacLean's, and she was there. We talked and danced. Nothing scandalous."

That was all Keli would get from me. The rest was private, and I wouldn't bend on that. I may have given Lumen up for Evanne, but I'd be damned if I let Keli tarnish my memories. Even the ones that were a mite embarrassing for me.

"Now," I said, "I'm going to go read to our daughter. I'll clean up from the meal since you prepared it. You can go back to your hotel now."

I walked away without waiting for a response because I wasn't sure how I'd take anything she said at this moment. Less than twenty-four hours and I was already second-guessing my decision. Only the reminder of the little girl waiting for me to read her a story kept me from going back and telling Keli we'd work things out through a lawyer. It was enough.

It had to be enough.

TWENTY-FOUR

LUMEN

"Lumen?"

I looked up to see a concerned-looking Siobhan standing in my doorway. After my awkward Monday, things had quieted back down even though Harvey was back. It seemed everyone had found juicier gossip fodder, though I hadn't inquired what.

"Yes?"

"Principal McKenna wants to see you in his office." She hesitated, then added, "Vice Principal Harvey is there too."

Shit.

Shit.

Shit.

I didn't let any of my concern show on my face. It

wasn't easy, but I managed. "Thank you. I'll head right down."

I waited until she left before I closed my eyes and reigned in the panic flooding my system. I'd thought when I'd made it through Tuesday and Wednesday without a word from Principal McKenna or Harvey that he'd decided to let things go. Apparently, I hadn't been as lucky as I'd thought.

The clicking of my shoes on the hallway tile as I made my way to the office seemed louder than usual, as if calling everyone's attention to me. *Come stare at the teacher who slept with a parent who then punched the vice principal...then dumped her two days later.*

I didn't let my pity party last. I hadn't done anything wrong. Not technically. I'd met and first slept with Alec before I'd learned about his daughter being in my class. I probably should have disclosed to Principal McKenna that Alec and I had been dating, but I hadn't broken any rules by not doing it. And I hadn't asked Alec to punch Vice Principal Harvey. That was on both of the men. Harvey, for not accepting my *no,* and Alec, for not letting me fight my own battles.

"I was told Principal McKenna wanted to see me," I said as I stopped at Alice's desk.

"They're expecting you. Go ahead in." Her expression gave nothing away.

I squared my shoulders and lifted my chin. I had nothing to be ashamed of or to apologize for. I'd kept my mouth shut about Harvey's behavior because I hadn't wanted to make waves. If he thought he could intimidate me into silence while still getting me into trouble about what Alec had done, he was about to see a whole new side of me.

"Ms. Browne," Principal McKenna greeted me. "Please, have a seat."

I took one of the seats across from the principal. Harvey stood behind him, a smug smile on his face. The bruise on his cheek was only noticeable because I knew what to look for, and I wondered if he'd used makeup to try to cover it.

"I'll get right to the matter at hand," Principal McKenna said. "It's been brought to my attention that, prior to coming here, you worked at a massage parlor."

All the air went out of the room. Of all the things I thought this meeting could be about, *that* wasn't even close to being on my radar. Realizing my jaw had dropped, I snapped it shut, brain scrambling to find footing.

"You lied on your resumé."

I shook my head. "All of my previous employment is on there."

"It says here that you worked at the front desk at

Real Life Bodywork." Vice Principal Harvey held up a piece of paper.

"We assumed that was a gym." Principal McKenna frowned.

I wanted to tell them both that their assumption wasn't my problem. I hadn't lied, and if they hadn't reached out or researched before hiring me, it was on them, not me.

I couldn't say any of that, though, not that way. Not if I wanted to keep my job. Since Kurt Wright wasn't a public school, termination of employees didn't have as much red tape as a unionized public school, and since it wasn't a religiously affiliated school, there'd been no 'morality' clause that would have given them cause had I previously worked at a strip club or something like that. I'd done nothing illegal and, when it came to my job, I hadn't even done anything someone could consider 'immoral.'

That didn't mean they wouldn't try to find a way to fire me simply for appearance's sake. They couldn't say that was why or I could sue them, but if I stepped over the line even in the slightest, I had little doubt they'd use it as an excuse to end my employment.

I chose my words carefully. "Real Life Bodywork is a legitimate massage parlor with employees licensed in massage. The owner is Lihua Jin, and she'll be happy to answer any questions you might have."

Both men still looked skeptical, but that wasn't really a surprise. I knew all too well the sort of thoughts that were immediately associated with the term 'massage parlor.'

"This says you worked at the desk," Harvey continued. "The person who reported this to us said that you personally offered massages. After hours, perhaps?"

He made the last three words a question, but I knew that was just for Principal McKenna's sake. Men like Harvey only saw women as objects divided into two categories: fuckable or not. He'd decided I was the former and saw this as justification for how he'd been treating me.

"My official job was working the desk," I explained, refusing to let him get a rise out of me. "But I did go through the necessary courses to become a licensed masseuse so I could pick up extra hours or substitute for another employee if need be. I can show you my certification if you like."

Principal McKenna studied me carefully and then leaned back in his chair. "Is the contact information on your resumé correct?"

"It is." I hoped this meant he'd at least call Lihua before making a decision.

"And if I do an internet search, I won't find anything...untoward regarding your place of employment?"

"No. The Jins run a reputable establishment."

"Then why would someone feel the need to report you?" Harvey asked, color creeping up his neck. "If you did nothing wrong, then why hide it?"

"I didn't hide it," I said, my voice calmer than how I felt. "And I don't know why someone would 'report' it. Perhaps they wanted to make sure I was honest about my work history, and they misunderstood the sort of place I worked."

Even as I said it, I knew it was a lie. Only one person connected to the school knew not only where I'd worked, but the fact that I'd given massages a few times. Unless someone had happened to see me both at Real Life Bodywork and here and made an assumption, there was only one person who could have shared that information.

Alec.

The heartache I'd been trying to deny merged into anger and betrayal, hurt that someone who I'd thought cared about me had tried to get me fired. There would have been no other reason for the report. I'd taken his 'we need to take a break' without a complaint. I'd seen Keli more than once and never behaved in anything but a professional and polite manner. I treated Evanne the same as I had before. I didn't spread rumors about him.

Why had he done this to me? Did he feel like he had to destroy me in order to prove to Keli he wanted her? Or was he simply that cruel and I hadn't seen it?

I could feel tears burning my eyelids as the truth of the matter set in.

Alec wasn't who I'd thought he was, and he'd never cared about me the way I had about him. When it came down to it, he was like the majority of the people I'd met in my life. Selfish, petty, and mean.

I wouldn't make that mistake again.

TWENTY-FIVE

ALEC

WHEN KELI SAID HER FRIENDS HAD INVITED HER TO go out with them for dinner and dancing, I hadn't even hesitated to encourage her to go. I wondered if she was testing me, wanting to see how I would react, but I'd been eager enough for a night without her that I hadn't bothered to try to figure it out. Now that I was cleaning up after the dinner Evanne and I had made, however, I was thinking about it.

Had she perhaps wanted to see if I'd be jealous? Tell her that I didn't want her dancing with other men? Or ask her to stay because I wanted to spend more time with her? Maybe she was testing to see what she could do if we had a relationship again.

Before, she'd had my weekends free, and she'd never complained about needing more time. She might have thought my expectations would be different if we lived together again.

Only I didn't think that would be a problem because this wasn't going to work. It couldn't. I didn't like her. It was that simple. Not being physically attracted to her was the least of it. The more time I spent with her, the more I remembered how much her personality had always grated on me.

She was an artist when we first met and still blamed me for her career not taking off. According to her, she would have been in the Louvre years ago had she not become pregnant. Because she never transferred that blame to Evanne, I didn't challenge her on it. From moment one, I'd given her enough money every month that she could simply pursue an art career, whether she made money at it or not.

I was willing to do that again.

What I wasn't willing to do was pretend that she and I could ever be a couple. I couldn't do it. I didn't enjoy spending time with her. I didn't want to talk to her about anything other than Evanne, and only then because I didn't want to take Evanne's mother from her. We had been amicable for eight years, and I would hold no bitterness or anger for how she'd handled things when she'd moved to Italy.

But amicable was all I could find myself willing to give. And if she kept pushing, even that might vanish.

"Daddy, can you come help me?" Evanne asked from the table where her homework was spread out.

"One moment." I finished rinsing suds from a pan and put it on the rack to dry.

Tonight, after I put Evanne to bed, I would take an uninterrupted look at my options. I would weigh the pros and the cons, both to Evanne and to me, and determine what the best course of action would be from here. Keli would be over tomorrow to take Evanne shopping for new shoes, and I would speak to her then. I knew she was hoping I would invite her to move into the house, even if it was into one of the many guest rooms, but I didn't believe that if she lived here, she'd be willing to accept that I wasn't interested in pursuing a relationship with her. It would be best for me to tell her that, once she found an apartment, we would negotiate the child support I would pay.

And I would tell her that we would not be going back to the same custody arrangement as before. I had only just realized how much I had missed when I'd given up an equal split of Evanne's time, thinking that my greatest contribution to her life was money. Never again.

I dried my hands and walked over to the table. As I

sat next to her, I asked, "How can I help you, *mo chride?*"

"We're starting fractions, and Ms. Browne said we have to learn how to do the work before she'll teach us how to put it in a calculator." Evanne heaved a sigh. "I told her that if she just showed us how to do it on a calculator, we could skip everything else because phones have calculators, and we'll always have phones, but she said we needed to learn it, anyway."

Dammit, Lumen.

"She's right," I agreed. "We may think we will always have phones, but technology breaks, does it not?"

"Yeah." Another heavy sigh. "It's just so boring."

I could think of a few other adjectives to describe it, but not ones I could share with my daughter. I rubbed the palms of my hands on my pant legs and scooted my chair closer to hers so I could look at the math sheet with her.

"All right, *mo chride.* Show me."

TWENTY-SIX
LUMEN

"I honestly don't know what to say to that."

Mai's response did nothing to make things any better. After a week of watching Keli pick up Evanne and an empty weekend with nothing to do but grade papers and clean, I'd hoped things would get better. Yesterday hadn't been any little bit better.

Today had been downright awful.

"I mean, I thought you'd had an awful week, but today..." She shook her head. "I couldn't imagine it. Probably why it's a good thing I'm not a teacher."

I rolled my eyes. "Yes, Mai. It's a good thing you're not a teacher."

"How did you handle it? I mean, any kid being upset over a bad grade would be hard, but the kid whose dad you dated?"

I winced as I remembered the way Evanne's face had crumpled when she'd seen the red marks on her homework. It hadn't been an actual grade, but I'd marked what was wrong so that the kids could follow along while I showed the correct work and answers on the board. Evanne hadn't spoken up in class after she'd gotten the paper back, not ask a question or to answer one.

It had broken my heart.

"You're a stronger woman than me," Mai said, her usual humor absent. "I mean it, Lumen. I don't know how you're doing it."

I wanted to pretend that she was just talking about teaching, but I knew she'd seen just how much the break-up had hurt me. How much it hurt for me to have to see Evanne and Keli every day. I knew Mai had seen it, but I didn't want to talk about it.

A loud bang on the door made us both jump.

"Lumen!"

My eyes went wide. "Alec?" It came out as a whisper.

He pounded on the door. "Dammit! Open the door!"

Mai was up and on her way to the door before I could completely process the fact that normally reserved Alec McCrae sounded angry at me.

"Where is she?" he demanded as soon as Mai opened the door.

I stood, and his gaze landed on me. Mai was still between us and didn't move, even when he took a step forward.

"How could you do it?"

Now, I could hear the hurt in his voice, and despite it all, it hurt me. "It's okay, Mai. Let him in."

She turned without moving. "Are you sure?"

I nodded. "Think you can go to Hob's or your mom's for a while?"

She just stood there, clearly deciding what to do before taking her purse and jacket from the nearby hook then stepping out of Alec's way. When he made to move past her, she put a hand on his arm.

"If you hurt her in any way, no one will find your body." Her fingers flexed on his arm, and I had no doubt that she'd have drawn blood if he'd been wearing short sleeves. "They, however, might find your cock bronzed on my trophy case."

If the circumstances had been any different, I might've found that funny.

She looked at me. "If you need me, call."

"I will."

Alec waited until the door closed before coming toward me. He was quiet now, but fury still burned in his eyes. I held my ground, chin up. I'd done nothing wrong. Hell, I hadn't even confronted him about telling the school about the massage parlor.

"How could you do that?" He stopped just out of arm's reach. "Evanne locked herself in her room when she got home, and when I went to see her after work, I found her crying about a bad grade on her math homework."

I opened my mouth to explain to him that I'd marked everyone's homework the same way, but he didn't let me get a word in.

"I'd thought you might be cold to Keli or me, but I never imagined that you would take out your feelings about the break-up on a child!"

I took a step back, the pain of his accusation almost physical.

"I will not stand for my daughter to be attacked simply because–"

"Enough!" I barely raised my voice, but it stopped him, anyway. "How. Dare. You."

My voice shook, and I could feel tears threatening, but the emotion came from anger more than anything else. This man I'd thought knew me intimately was accusing me of something truly awful.

I pointed my finger at him. "I am her *teacher*, you fucking bastard, and I treated her the same as every other child in my class. For you to say I allowed personal feelings to not only affect my teaching but actually take it out on an eight-year-old is..." I searched my mind for a strong enough word, "reprehensible."

"You—"

"No!" I snapped. "You came to my *home*! You're the one who made this personal, not me! If you have a problem with my teaching, then you speak to me at the school, like the professional I am."

"You made her cry!"

"You don't think I hate every time I have to give back a paper with wrong answers marked?" I was close to tears myself. "But it's part of being a teacher. If I don't correct them, how will they learn?"

I stopped suddenly and took a step back. I shook my head.

"You know what, I don't know why you've decided that ending things with me wasn't enough, but I'm not going to be bullied by some rich asshole who thinks he can do whatever he wants, and no one can touch him." I pointed at the door. "Get out."

TWENTY-SEVEN

ALEC

How did things get so out of control so fast?

I had to admit that coming here had been a mistake, but when Keli had told me that Evanne had seemed upset when she'd come home from school, and then I'd found her crying, her homework crumpled up in her hand...I snapped. My little girl had been hurting, and I'd needed to make it right.

Now, I saw that the way I had done things had been wrong, but I had no way of stopping what I had put into motion.

"I'll leave," I said, "but I'm going to speak to Principal McKenna about this. Evanne is smart, and there's no reason she should have done so poorly on a piece of homework."

Lumen's eyes flashed. "I always give my students the

chance to ask questions, and if Evanne doesn't understand something, she asks. I can't read minds."

"Then how do you explain the mistakes?"

"I wasn't there when she did the work," Lumen reminded me. "I encourage my students to ask for help from their parents for homework. If she doesn't ask for help—"

"She did!" I snapped. "She asked for my help!"

And that was when it hit me.

Fuck.

The blood drained from my face as I remembered sitting down Friday evening to help Evanne with her math homework.

Without a calculator.

I put out my hand to steady myself as the enormity of what I'd done hit me. This went far beyond Evanne getting poor marks on homework – which was bad enough – but I had said so many hurtful things to a woman who had done nothing but love and care for my daughter from the moment they'd first met.

"Alec?"

The concern in Lumen's voice made me look up.

"You look like you're going to pass out." She gestured to a nearby chair. "Sit. The last thing I need is you to fall, bash your head, then sue me on top of everything else."

I didn't tell her that would never happen. Instead, I

sat down. I needed to tell her the truth. It was the only way I could possibly begin to make up for what I had just done. I just didn't know if I could manage to stand while doing it. I wasn't simply humiliated, I was sick to my stomach, to borrow an American phrase.

"I helped her," I admitted quietly. I kept my gaze on the floor. "She asked for help and explained that you didn't want them to use calculators, which meant I couldn't use one."

Lumen came close enough for me to see her bare feet.

I closed my eyes and revealed something no one outside of my family knew. "I'm dyslexic. I can barely read or do math without a calculator or computer program."

TWENTY-EIGHT

LUMEN

I had to admit, out of all the possible things I could have imagined Alec saying, this wasn't even close to being on my radar. As soon as he said it, however, so many things made a lot more sense, not the least of which were Evanne's homework issue and Alec's irritation at going to a new restaurant for dinner.

"I struggled in primary school," he continued, the internal struggle he still felt coming out in his voice. "But I hid it well enough that I was nearly seven before Ma realized what was wrong. She helped me until she passed, and that year, the teachers felt for me enough they were laxer than they would have been otherwise."

He'd been Evanne's age when his mother died, I realized suddenly. I couldn't imagine having a student in my class who not only lost his mother but had five younger siblings to help out with as well.

"When we moved to San Ramon, Da enrolled us in a good private school, one that had specialty tracks for kids like me. I had a teacher there, Mr. Woodard, who taught me how to use the parts of my intelligence that were above average to not only get by, but to excel."

This was the most I'd ever heard Alec say at once, and certainly more than he'd ever told me about himself. The walls he'd used to keep me out were crumbling.

"By the time I was ready for grade nine, I transferred to the mainstream track with the rest of my siblings and graduated at the top of my class. I went to college, and no one there knew about my...issues. Then I received my degree, and Da made me a part of MIRI, and still, no one knew." He raised his head and finally let his eyes meet mine. "When Evanne was born, I bought the audio versions of the five most popular kids' books and memorized them. Every year, I'd memorize more, all so I could pretend to read to my daughter."

When he'd said his family was the only ones who knew, I'd assumed that had included Keli and Evanne, but now, I didn't think that was the case.

"I've been so careful," he said, "but helping Evanne with her homework wasn't something I had time to plan for, not to this extent, anyway. The math sheet on Friday

218

caught me off-guard, and I didn't know what to do except hope for the best." He rubbed his jaw, anguish in his eyes. "I never imagined it would come to this."

"You have to tell Evanne," I said softly.

"I can't." His tone was almost pleading. "How can I tell my daughter that I'm the reason her answers were wrong, and it was all because I can barely read?"

"She already knows at least part of it," I ventured. "She knows you helped her, but that I said the answers weren't correct. If I was to guess, she's more upset because she can't figure out what happened than she is about the marks themselves. There are far too many possibilities about why so many things were wrong, and she doesn't know how to ask, or who to ask."

"*Shite.*"

"You need to come clean with her, and I'll take some time tomorrow to have her go over some problems with me to make sure she understands what she's doing."

He nodded and closed his eyes for a moment. "I fucked up."

I decided that silence was better than agreeing with him because he might not have been thinking of all the same things I was. Just because he realized he'd been an ass about Evanne's homework didn't mean he thought us taking a break had been a bad idea.

He opened his eyes again and stood, the space

between us instantly charging. "There are no words to describe how much I regret speaking to you the way I did a few minutes ago. I am truly sorry for everything I said."

"Thank you." The words sounded stiff, but it wasn't because I didn't want to accept his apology. He wasn't the only one who didn't know how to put his feelings into words.

He came a step closer, his tone softening. "And I regret ending things between us. A week with Keli around was more than enough to show me that I'd made a terrible mistake."

I swallowed hard and told the hope inside me to stay inside that little box. Just because he regretted it didn't change a damn thing.

Yet.

"I told you that my mother died when I was young, and Theresa is my stepmother, but I didn't tell you how difficult it was for me to accept her. I love her, and we're family now, but a part of me will always wonder how different things could have been if my mother hadn't died."

I thought I knew where he was going with this, but I didn't interrupt. Assumptions had done enough damage already.

"When Keli came back from Italy after the shooting,

she told me that she wanted the three of us to be a family. I didn't agree because I wanted her back. I agreed to try because I thought that would be best for Evanne. That the best interest of my daughter would be served by having her parents together again."

Any child psychologist could have told him that staying together for the kids – or getting back together, in this case – would not end well for anyone involved. For Evanne's sake more than anyone else's, I hoped Alec was about to tell me that he and Keli had figured that out already.

"I should have told Keli that we were still as incompatible as we had been eight years ago." He shook his head. "The image I've had in my head of what a perfect family should be is a child's fantasy that I thought I had outgrown years ago."

He reached out and brushed back some hair that had fallen into my eyes. It was all I could do not to lean into his touch. Despite it all, I wanted him. Physically, I could have justified it. The man was smoking hot, and the sex was amazing. But it wasn't only the physical I wanted.

"I've missed you, *mo nighean bhan*."

My heart gave a leap at his words, at the endearment, but I couldn't just fall into his arms. Not when there was something I still needed him to explain.

I'd intended to let it go, but now he was here, in my apartment, telling me that breaking up with me had been a mistake and that he missed me. I wanted so badly to believe him, and I could forgive accusations driven by a combination of an overprotective father's love and the secret he considered shameful, but I couldn't move past one particular thing without an explanation.

"Why did you tell the school that I worked in a massage parlor?"

His eyebrows shot up, the surprise on his face genuine as far as I could tell. "What?"

"I was called into the principal's office last Thursday and asked why I'd lied on my resumé about my previous place of employment. I didn't, but they'd assumed it was a gym rather than doing their own research." I watched his face closely, looking for any sign of deception. "Someone called the school and told them that I used to give massages at a massage parlor, and we both know the sort of assumptions that come from a statement like that."

"*Shite.*"

My heart fell as recognition came into his eyes.

"It wasn't me, lass." He looked torn. "The other night, at dinner, Keli said something about how I probably wasn't the only parent you hit on at parent-teacher conferences–"

"She said *what?*"

"I told her that wasn't what happened," he said quickly. "I said we'd met before school started, and she wanted to know how. I wasn't going to tell her, but then she said she'd ask you and I didn't want to put you in that situation. I just told her that I'd been looking for a massage for sore muscles, and then I'd seen you again at MacLeans. I swear, I dinnae say anything else. Keli must've called the school and told them that bit."

I wasn't thrilled that he'd told Keli, but it sounded like he hadn't given her the full story. Since it would've shown him in a worse light than me, it made sense. It wasn't his fault that she'd tried to screw me over at work with it. I'd already had the impression that she wasn't fond of me. This just solidified it.

"I'll talk to her. She'll leave you be," he promised. "Are you in trouble?"

"No. I hadn't lied about it, and I told them if they called, Lihua would vouch for the respectability of the business."

"It would probably make things worse if I talked to Principal McKenna, wouldn't it?"

I gave him a soft smile. "It would, but I appreciate your willingness to do so."

He put his hand on my cheek, his thumb leaving a trail of heat where it brushed across my skin. "Is it too late, lass? Have I broken too much between us? Is there any chance we can fix this?"

I put my hand over his and then turned my head to kiss his palm. "No, it's not too much to be fixed. Relationships aren't perfect. We just have to be willing to put in the work."

He tipped my chin up so our eyes could meet. "I want to put in the work, lass. I want this."

"Good." I leaned toward him and brushed my lips across his. "That's what I want too."

His hands went to my waist, tugging me against his body as he bent his head and took my mouth in a scorching kiss that threatened to burn me up from the inside out. I grabbed the front of his shirt, flicking my tongue out to meet his.

Damn, I'd missed this.

TWENTY-NINE
ALEC

I COULDN'T BELIEVE HOW CLOSE I'D COME TO LOSING this, to losing *her*. The thought made me tighten my grip on her, made my exploration of her mouth rougher, needier. After a week without her, my body ached for hers with a desperation I'd never known with another woman. I wouldn't push her into anything, but if she was willing...

"I need you, lass." I broke from the kiss only long enough to say the words, and then my lips were back on hers. When I felt her stretching to reach me, I lifted her, and she wrapped her legs around me.

"Yes," she breathed against my mouth. Her teeth scraped my bottom lip. "Bedroom."

The rush of relief that went through me almost as strong as my desire. I kicked off my shoes and somehow managed to shrug out of my jacket before heading for the short hallway that led to Lumen's bedroom. She squirmed in my arms, her hands moving across my shoulders, my back, up my neck. Fingers in my hair, nails scratching my scalp. Each roll of her hips put near-painful pressure on my cock, but I wouldn't have traded it for anything short of being inside her.

I lowered her to the bed, unwilling to release her just yet. The angle was awkward with how small her bed was, but I didn't care about any of that. She cradled me between her legs, her arms trying to pull me closer, as if that were even possible. Her hands tugged at the back of my shirt, teeth nipping at my bottom lip, desperate tension radiating from every cell. She made a frustrated noise, and the sound made me smile. Then her hands were pushing rather than pulling, and I froze, worried that I'd crossed some line.

I shot up, my feet finding the floor even as my knees rested on the edge of the mattress.

"I'm sorry, lass. Did I hurt you?"

"No, no." She sat up, reaching for my hands. She brought them up and kissed the knuckles on one, then the other. "You didn't hurt me. I just wanted your damn shirt off."

It took a moment for the words to sink in, and then a

laugh burst out of me. "Daft, woman. I thought I'd done something wrong."

She went up on her knees and reached for the front of my shirt. "Not wrong. You're just wearing too many clothes." Color flooded her cheeks. "You're always wearing too many clothes."

And just like that, the humor was gone.

"Aye, lass." My voice was rough. "I ken the feeling well."

As she undid my buttons, I kept my hands at my sides despite the nearly overwhelming urge to tear her clothes off. I'd have my turn soon enough. For the moment, though, I enjoyed watching her. Then again, I always enjoyed watching her.

The little crease between her eyebrows when she concentrated. How her lips parted ever so slightly when she was aroused. Heat from her fingers as they brushed my skin. The hard points of her nipples that told me she wasn't wearing a bra under her over-sized cotton tee.

"You're fucking gorgeous," she said as she pushed my shirt off my shoulders. Her hands burned paths down my chest and stomach, my muscles flexing and jumping under her touch.

"Is that so?"

"It is." She turned me around and began tracing the cross that covered most of my back. She'd seen it before, but never examined it with the intense focus I felt now. "S.A.M.?"

She made it a question, and it was one I didn't mind answering. "Shannon Allen McCrae."

"Your mother." Her lips pressed against the spot where the initials had been inked.

"Aye."

Her arms slid around my waist, fingers splayed over my chest. "You're a good man, Alec McCrae. Your mother would be proud of you."

I closed my eyes, Lumen's words striking deeper than I would've thought possible. Da had said similar things to me. When I'd graduated high school and again when I'd graduated from college. When Evanne had been born. He had told me how proud and how happy Ma would have been with what I had done with my life.

I wasn't as certain that was the truth.

To have someone like Lumen see me, *truly* see me, both the good and the bad...and then have her tell me that I was a good man and that my mother would be proud. Even after the assumptions I made and the way I'd handled them.

"I can hear you thinking too hard." Her hands slid down to the waist of my pants. "Did I completely kill the mood?"

I turned in her arms and dipped my head to touch my lips to hers. "Not at all, *mhurninn*."

The hands at the small of my back moved down to grab my ass. "Good, because I definitely like it better when you get me off than when I have to do it alone."

The flood of images that inundated my mind at that statement had me instantly and painfully hard. "At some point, lass, I'm going to want you to demonstrate that difference." I slid my hands under her shirt and up to move my thumbs across her nipples. "But later. Because right now, I need to make you come. Hard."

Lumen's eyes widened, and she caught her breath. Whatever she'd thought I would say, that hadn't been it. She nodded and then raised her arms. I pulled her shirt over her head and tossed it aside, more interested in those tight peach-colored nipples and firm breasts than I was where her shirt went.

"Lay down."

She did as I instructed, yanking off her pants as she moved. With her spread out in front of me like a vision, I had to reach down and adjust myself. She made me doubt my self-control, and not much in the world could manage that.

I went to my knees on the floor next to the bed and used her legs to pull her to the edge. She let out a startled laugh, and the sound made me smile. Her joy was as intoxicating as her arousal, something I wouldn't have thought possible. When I draped her legs over my shoulders, the light on her face and the sparkle in her eyes deepened somehow, leaving me speechless.

The things this woman made me feel.

I kissed the inside of one thigh, then the other, worrying at the skin with my teeth until I left a mark. My mark. Satisfied, I turned my attention to more sensitive skin. I ran my tongue along the outside of her lips, then delved between them, tasting all of the flavors that were uniquely Lumen.

"Alec," she breathed out my name, back arching off the bed.

I gripped her hips tighter and moved with her, relentlessly driving her toward climax. Each sound she made, each time her muscles clenched or her eyes closed were all signals to guide me to what would get her there faster or what would slow her down. These were the things I could read, a place my disability couldn't touch.

She was close, her hands scrabbling against her bedspread, fisting the fabric, nails digging in. Her eyes were closed, sensual lips parted. Each panting breath drew my attention to her breasts. Her skin glistened with sweat, and I felt her muscles quivering as she strained toward release.

One day, I would have enough patience to tease her,

draw out experience by taking her to the edge, and denying her time and again, making her sob and beg.

But today was not that day.

I pulled her clit into my mouth, holding it between my teeth as I sucked on it. She cried out, her eyes flying open. Wild, they caught mine, and my cock throbbed at the promise in those azure depths.

"Oh...Alec..."

A shudder went through her, and then I felt her come, muscles tensing, a look of near surprise turning into one of pure ecstasy. I helped her ride the wave of pleasure, easing back bit by bit until her body went limp, and only then did I pull back.

My own legs were weak as I stood, my cock chafing against my soft cotton boxer-briefs. I kept my gaze on her as I removed the rest of my clothes, drinking in the sight of her sprawled limbs, the flush to her fair skin, the look of utter satisfaction on her face. It wasn't until I reached into my pants pocket that I realized what I hadn't brought with me.

"Condom?"

If she didn't have one, we'd work around it, but that wouldn't be my first choice.

"Still in the drawer." She pointed.

I wanted to ask if that meant she'd kept them in the hopes that I would come back to her, or if she simply hadn't wanted to waste them and had intended to use them with the next man. Even as I thought it, I had to admit that I didn't actually want to know the answer to that. The thought of her with another man made my stomach twist with jealousy.

By the time I finished putting on the condom, I'd pushed those thoughts from my mind and was back to being entirely focused on her. She'd pushed herself up the bed enough that I now had room, and I wasted no time settling myself between her legs.

I propped myself on one arm, giving myself the balance to kiss her while my free hand was busy between us, moving the head of my cock back and forth between her lips, gathering moisture. Her fingernails scraped over my nipple, and I groaned at the zing of pleasure that went through me.

"Ready, lass?"

"For you, always." She reached up to pull my face back down to hers as I pushed into her.

Her body rose to meet mine, and we locked together like two puzzle pieces. She wrapped her legs around me, heels resting on my thighs, and her hands moved to my shoulders, then my arms, fingers tightening as she rocked against me, sounds of frustration telling me it was time to move.

Torturing myself as much as her, I took my time

pulling out. Then, raising my head so I could watch her, I surged forward, burying myself again with a single smooth stroke. She gasped, eyes widening.

"Again."

I smiled. "As you command, lass."

Over and over I drove into her, never rushing, never stopping. The air between us thickened, and the world faded away. I drowned in her eyes, reveled in her body, and hoped that I could give her all the pleasure she deserved. When it began to be too much, I increased my pace, and she matched it, our bodies coming together harder and faster until we finally exploded, her only seconds behind me, and all we could do was cling to each other and ride it out together.

THIRTY

LUMEN

"Fuck! I have to go!"

That certainly wasn't the reaction I'd expected after mind-blowing sex less than ten minutes ago. I tried not to be hurt as I grabbed my blanket to cover myself.

Then, suddenly, Alec was there, crouching by the edge of the bed, stark naked but completely unselfconscious about it. He put his hands over mine, his expression serious.

"Believe me, lass, the last thing I want is to leave you alone in that bed, but I'm already enough of a shite father for thinking with my cock instead of remembering my little girl's at home, upset."

Understanding hit me, and I immediately shook my head. "You're a great father, Alec. You made a mistake based on something that's been hurting you for a long time, and you weren't in any condition to explain things to her. You needed...time."

He didn't look like he believed me, but I'd noticed that he was one of those people who tended to be harder on himself than on others.

"Thank you." He gave me a stiff smile. "You gave me time, *mo nighean bhan*. But I need to tell Evanne the whole truth, and she deserves to hear it face-to-face."

I leaned forward and kissed his forehead. "I was right. You are a good man."

He cupped my chin and gave me a soft kiss. "I'm going to speak with Keli as well. She and I will come up with an arrangement for custody of Evanne, but it won't be including anything to do with her and me. You're the only one I want a relationship with, lass."

My heart felt like it would burst out of my chest. "I want that too."

He ran his thumb along my bottom lip. "The wisest thing we could do would be to take this slow, but I cannae leave you here like this without making certain you know that I'm not taking this lightly. I've never been more serious about anyone."

I could barely breathe. I could hardly believe this was happening.

"In fact, I want you to move in with me."

My jaw dropped.

He smiled. "Sudden, lass, I know. And I dinnae need an answer now. Whenever you feel ready, however long it takes. I just needed you to know that I've made my decision."

When he'd stormed in here an hour ago, this was not where I'd seen my night going. My heart and my libido wanted to answer the invitation, to tell him I'd love to live with him. My brain, however, knew that it'd be a better idea to wait and make sure this wasn't simply a great sex thing.

"As I said, I don't need an answer right now." He stood. "But I do need to get home to talk to Evanne."

"Of course. Go. Be a great dad." I rolled onto my back and watched him find his clothing.

The warmth inside my belly curled into something pleasant as I thought about what he'd said and what it meant. Even though I didn't know exactly when I'd feel ready to accept his invitation, I would be there one day. Probably sooner rather than later. And I'd have a home. A family.

Now fully dressed, Alec leaned down and kissed me. Gentle. Sweet. Full of promise.

"Sleep well, lass." He caressed my cheek. "I'll see myself out."

I nodded and watched him walk out. It was okay

that he was leaving me alone right now because we weren't done.

We were just getting started.

THE END

Don't miss the exciting ending to Alec and Lumen's story in *Mending Fate*, The Scottish Billionaire Book 3.

Printed in Great Britain
by Amazon